"I like my women with experience."

Stephen's taunting words were the last straw. Laurel raised her hand in a blind fury only to have it caught in ruthless fingers.

"I'm not a little girl," Laurel protested scathingly. "I am a schoolteacher, you know."

"Oh?" Stephen mocked, as he pulled her closer. "Then perhaps you should teach me what you know. Or shall I give you lesson number one?"

"I don't know what you're talking about," Laurel snapped angrily, attempting to jerk free.

"I'm talking about this—" His kiss bruised Laurel's lips and shattered her fury, leaving her confused and bewildered. "Put that under the heading of experience," Stephen said, amused.

"I will," Laurel answered defiantly. "Under the subheading of unpleasant!"

Teachers Must Learn

by

NERINA HILLIARD

Harlequin Books

TORONTO•LONDON•NEW YORK•AMSTERDAM
SYDNEY•HAMBURG•PARIS•STOCKHOLM

Original hardcover edition published in 1968
by Mills & Boon Limited

ISBN 0-373-01302-7

Harlequin edition published May 1969

Second printing August 1969
Third printing July 1972
Fourth printing January 1979
Fifth printing May 1979
Sixth printing August 1979

Printed in U.S.A.

CHAPTER ONE

LAUREL drew in her breath sharply, then let it out slowly in a sigh of sheer enchantment. The island, dreaming in the sunlight, cradled in sparkling waters and roofed with benevolent blue skies, was so unbelievably beautiful.

'It's like something out of a fairy tale,' she said softly.

Her companion, whose cynical gaze was also focussed upon the island, shrugged her elegant shoulders slightly.

'I thought that when I first came here,' she admitted. 'I suppose most people are slightly bowled over when they see Ladrana for the first time. But the pity is that one gets accustomed to places, and the magic fades.'

Laurel was affected by her cynicism in the same way that she was affected by the sudden lowering of the temperature on a hot summer's day. But she had not come all this way to have an otherwise magical moment marred by a lack of enthusiasm on the part of a fellow passenger aboard the small coastal freighter. So while Beryl Cornish disappeared inside the single public saloon behind them she went closer to the rail and gripped at it eagerly.

Beryl called out to her a trifle mockingly before she disappeared:

'Let's hope you'll find everything on Ladrana just what you expected. . . . And let's hope you'll always think of it as a fairytale island!'

Laurel frowned as she gazed out over the sparkling sea and the distance between her and her destination lessened with every passing second. Even now she was not sure whether she liked Beryl Cornish. Her cynicism was sometimes repellent, but for all that there was something vaguely attractive to the total inexperience Laurel somewhat ruefully knew to be hers in complete sophistication and rather world-weary confidence. It mocked at her own youthfulness, but it also seemed to hint at things, as yet undreamed of, that could be wildly exciting. Only she

5

hoped that if ever she discovered those things the result would not be total boredom, as in the case of Beryl Cornish.

For a very brief period she dwelt upon the possibility that she might one day, too, be jaded and slightly sad, and then she dismissed it as she recollected that this was the glorious present. For her the whole of life was breathlessly exciting, and round every corner that she encountered there was likely to be something new and completely fascinating. At any rate, from now on.

For twenty-two years she had been Laurel Shannon, to whom nothing very much had ever happened. She was labelled 'schoolmarm', which in itself seemed to preclude the possibility of anything out of the ordinary happening to her. Journeys to romantic parts of the world simply did not happen to girls in such prosaic occupations, even when they were still in their early twenties and were blessed with the trimmest and slenderest of figures, with the added accompaniment of tobacco brown hair that curled delightfully and naturally, a mouth that quirked upwards engagingly at its enchanting corners, and eyes that were neither blue nor green but some mysterious shade between the two set between long, curling eyelashes a few shades darker than her hair.

Laurel herself did not consider her physical appeal was very much more than average, but she did know that she had one important thing that was not likely to desert her for several years yet . . . the freshness of youth. And youth was a powerful weapon to possess when one had virtually nothing else. It meant that one could still look forward, and looking backward was not in the least painful. Anything and everything that happened was a novelty, and for that she was supremely grateful.

Her sea-green eyes continued to smile as she looked out over the sea, and she knew that the smile was largely due to the letter inside her handbag. She resisted the temptation to re-read it while the island was drawing so rapidly closer, for apart from the fact that it was not an ideal moment she already knew the contents of it off by heart.

'*Dear Brat,*' it began with affectionate insult, and continued in Kennedy's bubbling, irrepressible style. '*Believe it or not, the prodigal seems to have made good. Don't ask me how it happened, but the plantation is paying its way – and more – at last.*' There followed a long, incomprehensible description of the various pests that attacked tropical crops, lapsing at times into total illegibility, and concluded with the amazing information: '*I have forwarded enough to the London bank to cover your passage. A holiday away from the other brats will do you good, and I'm looking forward to showing you off to the chaps on the island. Don't let me down.*

Ned.'

P.S. *You might even make the redoubtable Stephen Barrington fall flat on his face.*'

Well, of course, she had no desire whatsoever to make this unknown Stephen Barrington fall flat on his redoubtable face, even if she had the ability, which she very much doubted, whatever he was like. From that postscript he sounded just a little aloof and perhaps even formidable. Something told her that Ned did not like him – or was not particularly sold on him, at any rate – and loyalty to her brother, whom she had always adored, set the hackles of antipathy bristling at the thought of a man she had never met, whom she had not the smallest desire to meet, and who obviously occupied a very low place in the esteem of the prospering Ned. When the moment arrived that brought them face to face she would probably look at him in such a way that he would realize immediately she had been warned in advance, and she hoped he was the type who could take a snub.

She was the friendliest soul when people were friendly to her, but she didn't want any man falling for her who apparently found it difficult to fall for other people.

The tap of high heels sounded behind her on the deck, and she turned from the rail with new purpose in her slender body, although she hoped it was disguised enough as she smiled up at Beryl Cornish.

The elder woman had thrown a light, matching linen coat over her sleeveless blouse and linen skirt. She was going on beyond Ladrana, but apparently intended to go ashore during the freighter's stay at the island.

Beryl leaned on the rail at her side, watching the feathery fronds of the island palms approach.

'How long is it since you last saw your brother?' she asked, without turning to look at the girl.

Laurel sighed, with a faraway look in her eyes. 'Over seven years.' She glanced up at the woman. 'I'm afraid we all thought he was quite crazy, wanting to come out here. Mother and Father were killed suddenly, in a train crash, while he was away. They would have loved to know he was successful in the end.'

Perhaps they did know, somehow. She hesitated a moment, then asked baldly, in complete change of subject:

'Who is Stephen Barrington?'

Beryl's pencilled eyebrows flickered upwards in surprise, then she lowered them over narrowed, cautious eyes.

'Now you're getting on dangerous ground, my child.' Her voice had a guarded drawl as she added, 'What do *you* know about Stephen Barrington?'

Laurel attempted to shrug nonchalantly. 'Nothing, except what I gathered from one sentence in my brother's letter.'

Something faintly mocking glowed in the other woman's eyes. There was a hint of warning in her tone, though, as she advised:

'Don't start getting interested in Stephen, my child. It wouldn't be wise, and for another thing, it might be dangerous – not that I think Stephen would really give you more than a passing glance,' she added, but Laurel somehow felt that the deliberate cruelty was not directed at herself, but at the world in general.

Nevertheless, her chin went up with unconscious pride and defiance.

8

'I have no particular interest in this Stephen Barrington, whoever he is. From what I've heard about him so far I don't find him at all likeable. I merely inquired because I gathered from his letter that Ned doesn't like him.'

'And you want to know what he's like, so you can be a loyal little sister and dislike him too?' Beryl suggested, but this time she was smiling without any unkindness. She was silent for a moment, frowning thoughtfully. 'It would be rather hard to say just what he's like, because I don't think any woman has ever really got underneath that mocking exterior of his. He's English, of course, but he's acquired quite a few Portuguese mannerisms, probably due to the fact that his family have lived out here for centuries. He owns over half the island, quite apart from holdings in other parts of the world,' she added casually, as if it was the man who had interested her to the exclusion of everything else, even the fabulous fortune he apparently possessed. 'I think that's about all I should tell you. You can make up your mind about the rest yourself.' She slanted a quizzical glance at the girl. 'I don't think you'll find it hard. Stephen has quite a forceful personality. He doesn't leave a person in doubt as to how they feel about him.'

She turned back to look out over the sea, at the fast approaching island, and Laurel forbore to ask any more questions, feeling that she had heard quite enough about this Stephen Barrington to make him sound rather detestable. In any case, Ned's judgment was rarely at fault.

Was that him there? She started and leaned forward eagerly over the rail. Surely nobody else would have that shock of blond hair. Yes, it was Ned. In quite uncontrollable excitement, she waved enthusiastically, bringing an amused and envious smile to the lips of the woman at her side.

'Your brother?'

'Yes.' Laurel threw her a swift, smiling glance and waved again to the figure on shore. This time the man started to vigorously return her greeting.

9

The ship pulled in at a weathered stone quay and she was able to clearly recognize the tall, blond man who was looking up at her with the familiar grin on his lips that had always, in the old days, managed to get her to do whatever he wished, from carrying his school books to helping clean down his first ramshackle old car.

Nevertheless, when at length she did step down on to the quay, their greeting was restrained, because both were naturally reticent in front of an audience. Only the fervent clasp of her brother's fingers on her own told Laurel how much the meeting meant to him as well.

One eyebrow, startlingly fair against the suntan of his face, jerked upwards quizzically.

'You've grown.'

'You'd expect me to, wouldn't you?' Laurel retorted, her mock indignation hiding her pleasure and excitement at seeing him again. 'After all, I was only fifteen when you left.'

The irrepressible grin that was no whit different from years ago turned his lips up at the corners.

'All right, don't nag me, schoolmarm,' he drawled. 'I'm not one of your inkstained and grubby little pupils.'

'My pupils were not grubby,' Laurel contradicted, but her eyes were smiling and saying how good it was to be with him, and his eyes were smiling down into hers and saying the same thing.

There seemed to be no difficulty with Customs on the island and very soon Laurel found her bags being transferred to a well-kept little car which stood outside the official port buildings. Ned drove slowly through the town, to give her a chance to indulge her desire to look round and goodnaturedly answered the questions that tumbled out like a pent-up flood. Once he did glance sideways at her with an amused grin.

'I somehow can't visualize you handling a bunch of rowdy youngsters.'

'They were not rowdy,' Laurel retorted, in instant defence of her class, yet nevertheless remembered young

Tommy Marsden, who invariably caused trouble of some sort immediately her back was turned. A bubbling laugh welled up, destroying all vestige of gravity. 'You haven't seen me when I'm really roused,' she added, completely contradicting her previous statement.

Ned grinned as he swung the car away from the last straggling buildings of the town and on to a side road, leaving the other better kept and smoother one to continue on into the mysterious depths of the island.

Clouds of dust rose from the dry ground as the car bumped over the ruts and penetrated even through the closed windows, so that the atmosphere became absolutely stifling and Laurel wondered whether it might not be better to open the window and at least have some air in the car, since they seemed doomed to have the dust in any case. She tried it, and hastily decided otherwise, aware of Ned's grin as she wound up the window again.

'You'll get used to the dust,' he informed her callously.

Laurel coughed and felt it tickling its way up her nose and did not think she would ever get used to it. At least, she knew she would never be able to say truthfully that she liked it.

They passed neatly set out rows of sisal and agrave and Ned informed her proudly that on the other side of the plantation were planted pawpaw, bananas and tea, as well as cotton.

Laurel threw him a puzzled, laughing glance. 'Do you grow everything here?'

'Nearly everything,' Ned replied, with an expansive wave of his hand that nearly sent them off the road and into a group of thatched, conical native huts, where naked piccanins played outside baked mud walls.

Beyond a grove of wide-branched tamarisk and mauve-flowering Judas trees, the house at last came into view, flanked by scarlet flowering gums and vivid flowers. The house itself was like some English cottage, defiantly nestling among tropical trees and flowers and looking quite pugnacious about it.

Laurel could not restrain an almost childish giggle. 'It looks as if it's going to pick a fight!'

'I've often thought that myself,' Ned agreed. 'It was built originally by a very belligerent Irishman, who would start up a fight at the drop of a hat. He must have left some of his personality behind.'

Laurel opened the door before he could cross to her side and stood looking round delightedly.

'I'm going to love living here, Ned,' she said with a happy sigh, and Ned grinned in that indulgent, affectionate way.

'I'll be seeing that you don't leave yet awhile, either.' He caught her hand and led her inside. 'Like it?'

Laurel nodded eagerly. The cottage was completely English inside except for the tropical flowers in a tall bronze vase that stood upon a stone pedestal, and had apparently left its belligerent Irish façade outside.

Ned led her through the rooms, pointing out different acquisitions with obvious pride of ownership, the gay curtains in the living room that he had bullied the native women into making, cushions on a leather couch that lay there like bright butterflies come to rest on its dark surface. Finally he took her through to the kitchen and introduced her to a middle-aged Portuguese woman, who bobbed a shy curtsey and roused two young coloured girls into frenzied activity with a flood of instructions in their own language, so that by the time Ned and Laurel had come down from upstairs, where she had been shown her own room, tea was laid for them in the delightfully cool dining room.

As Pepita went out, Ned indicated the tea-tray. 'Will you pour out? Now that I have a perfectly good sister here, I might as well make use of her!'

Laurel suddenly threw her arms around his neck and hugged him in an excess of youthful affection, feeling as if she had grown several years younger since coming to Ladrana. She could not possibly be the same person who had waxed stern to the impish Tommy Marsden.

'I'm going to love being here,' she said again.

Ned put his own arms around her and gently ruffled her hair. 'I'm going to love having you. Don't go leaving me too soon.'

'I beg your pardon.'

Both of them started as a voice spoke from the doorway. As Ned released her, Laurel turned quickly, feeling embarrassed to find a total stranger watching them from the doorway and, all in that one instant, decided that she did not at all care for eyes that were dark grey and held a distinctly mocking light. In fact she was conscious of a tingling along her spine that betokened the birth of antagonism, especially when the piercing eyes left her to go to Ned with an upward twitch of a jet black eyebrow that was positively diabolical.

Ned grinned, not in the least embarrassed, it seemed. 'Come in, Steve,' he invited. 'You're not interrupting any tender moment.'

As the newcomer left the doorway and came nearer, Laurel noticed that he somehow managed to dwarf the little room and overwhelm them with his height and arrogant assurance. Ned drew her forward, but she really did not need his introduction. She had already guessed who the man was.

'This is my sister, Laurel,' he said, and his smile was not at all the expression she had expected him to wear when introducing a man he disliked. 'Laurel – the great man of the island, Stephen Barrington,' he added with the grin that had won him so many friends.

Laurel held out her hand reluctantly and found it engulfed in the strong brown fingers of the man. A quick, all-encompassing glance took in his height and the dark, virile tan of his skin against which the parting of thin, cynical lips showed strong, white teeth. Added to that thin, aquiline features, thick black hair with a tendency to wave slightly, and those piercing dark grey eyes that seemed as if they could look right through you, into the secret recesses of mind and heart, made it simple for Laurel

13

to accept Beryl Cornish's opinion of this man. He was undoubtedly both dangerous and experienced, and far from likeable. He might improve on acquaintance, but she doubted it.

She withdrew her fingers somewhat hurriedly after his had closed round them. . . . Not that his seemed disposed to linger, but because she was afflicted all at once with a most unusual breathlessness, even while instinctive antagonism put a sparkle into the eyes that met his mocking grey glance.

'Of all things, believe it or not,' Ned put in, not apparently aware of the veiled hostility between them, 'she's a schoolmarm.'

Again that diabolical black brow jerked upwards in a fashion that made Laurel's fingers positively itch to strike that attractive, mocking face.

'You do indeed surprise me,' he murmured, watching her every change of expression. 'I thought schoolteachers wore their hair in buns, and were addicted to flat-heeled sensible shoes,' lowering his glance to her high-heeled, impractical but extremely smart white sandals.

Laurel attempted to shrug nonchalantly. 'You're a little behind the times, Mr. Barrington,' she commented. 'Those hallmarks went out with the industrial revolution.'

Ned pretended to shrink. 'Break it down, infant. Steve's not that old!'

He was not old at all, Laurel realized, probably in his early thirties, and the light tropical suit he wore so accentuated his tan and masculine attraction that it increased her antagonism in some strange way.

It was Pepita who saved the situation, appearing diffidently in the doorway to enquire whether the Senhor Stephen would be joining them for tea.

Ned sent him an enquiring glance. 'What about it, Steve? Will you join us?'

Laurel was quite sure that he was on the point of refusing, but her anticipatory look must have attracted his glance, for he smiled at her charmingly and said he would

14

love to stay to tea.

'I actually came over in order to let you know that Anthea has arranged a rather sudden dinner-party for tonight,' he explained to Ned, 'and we hope very much that you'll accept an invitation. Naturally, since Miss Shannon is now a member of your household, we'd like her to come along with you.'

Ned glanced at his sister.

'What do you say, brat?'

She shrugged again.

'It's up to you to decide, Ned. . . .'

'Perhaps, if you're too tired . . .?' Barrington began mockingly.

But Ned scoffed at the idea.

'Tired? Laurel? She hardly looks it, does she? And, by the way,' he continued, as he passed the visitor the cake, 'if you're going to keep on calling her Miss Shannon it's likely to lead to complications. She'll probably mistake you for a member of her class and treat you accordingly. Better make it Laurel, and she can call you Steve.'

The idea of Stephen Barrington being mistaken, even in a moment of mental aberration, for anything other than what he was brought a faint smile of disbelief to Laurel's lips. But at the same time she realized that he was waiting for her acceptance or otherwise of his invitation, and she was not entirely bereft of good manners. She smiled at him politely and said sweetly that she would love to dine with him and Anthea that night. She had no idea who Anthea was, but it sounded a very charming name.

Later she sat in front of her dressing-table mirror and thoughtfully contemplated the somewhat intriguing problem of Stephen Barrington . . . whom she had permission to call Steve.

It was quite clear to her that she disliked him, but for some extraordinary reason she found herself quite unable to stop thinking about him. Beryl had been right when she said he did not leave a person long in doubt of the way in which he affected them; but even when a decision had been taken to dislike him thoroughly there were still reservations. Or perhaps not so much reservations as an irritating ability he had of intruding his mental image on one's thoughts. It interfered completely with one's capacity for clear-thinking on any other subject, which was in itself infuriating.

A soft tap at her door interrupted her musing, and she swung round to call 'Come in' to her brother.

Ned entered looking surprisingly elegant in his dinner-jacket, which was of tropical white, and with his hair sleeked back and his chin close-shaved.

At the sight of her he pursed his lips in a silent wolf whistle.

'Well, well!' he exclaimed. His expression said volumes as he wandered round her, taking in every detail of her appearance. 'Well!' he exclaimed again, as if that one word constituted the sum total of his appreciative vocabulary.

'Holes with water in them,' Laurel replied with a gleaming smile.

Ned shook his head. 'No ... You can't possibly be a schoolteacher – not in that dress!'

Laurel directed at him a warning look.

'One of these days I'll give you a demonstration of what a peace-keeping martinet I can really be,' she promised him. 'You'll be surprised!' Then a warm smile flashed up into her eyes. 'But I haven't thanked you yet for giving me such a darling of a room, Ned,' she said. 'Not only is it a very feminine room, but the colour schemes are perfect. I had no idea you were so knowledgeable on such subjects.'

'As a matter of fact,' Ned admitted, 'it was Anthea who helped me choose the curtains, and that sort of thing. In fact, she chose everything, and put all the finishing touches to the room.'

Instantly Laurel's interest was alerted.

'Anthea?' she echoed. 'And who is Anthea?'

'Anthea Barrington.'

Something slightly discordant jangled at the base of Laurel's spine.

'You mean Stephen Barrington's wife?'

Ned shook his head and grinned in amusement at her mistake.

'His sister. Steve isn't married, and so far as I know not even contemplating marriage. He's the island's prize bachelor.'

Laurel made a disdainful sound.

'I pity the girl he eventually marries,' she declared with a venom that was unlike her. 'She'll probably find that he's not much of a prize after all.'

'Oh, I don't know.' Ned looked vaguely surprised. 'Steve's not a bad sort.'

'A girl would be unable to call her life her own married to him.'

Ned shook his head with such emphasis that it was Laurel's turn to feel surprise. She had not expected the practical Ned to champion another man so fervently.

'When old Steve falls for somebody he'll do it pretty hard and she'll probably be able to do just what she likes with him,' he predicted. 'At any rate, up to a point,' he added more dubiously, recollecting the other man's inflexible character.

'I doubt if he would ever fall in love,' Laurel mused. 'He wouldn't allow that insufferable assurance of his to be dented in any way, and even to acknowledge himself in love would be a sign of weakness on his part. Anyway,' giving her head a slight shake, 'why do we allow him to monopolize our conversation? There are other things to talk about . . . his sister, for instance. What's she like?'

Ned walked to the window and stared out into the softly scented night world of the garden. Although he didn't actually say anything to create the impression, Laurel suddenly conceived the idea that he was embarrassed.

'You'll see her for yourself tonight.'

'Is she as uncompromising as her brother?'

'Not a bit.'

'Is she nice?'

'*I* think she is.' He turned from the window, and pretended to be startled because it was later than he had supposed. 'Come on, we'd better get moving—'

'You like her, don't you, Ned?' Suddenly his sister was standing in front of him, and she was frankly curious because he had revealed so much. 'You like her very much?'

'Nonsense!'

'It isn't nonsense, because my sixth sense tells me it's true. Does she like you? . . . Is she in *love* with you?'

'Of course not.' He would have put her almost roughly aside, but she clung on to his arm.

'Tell me the truth, Ned.' She was half laughing, half insistent.

Impatiently he glared at her, and then he bowed his head before her superior will.

'Oh, well, if you must know the truth, I do rather like her. But Anthea is a flirt and there are lots of other fellows who like her as well. I've had the good sense not to let my feelings carry me away, and I long ago decided that I'd be mad if I asked her to marry me.'

'Why? Because of her flirtatious tendencies?'

He made an impatient movement.

'No, because she's Anthea Barrington.'

'What difference does that make?' But she was beginning to understand, and she didn't really need him to underline her sudden knowledge for her.

'What difference?' He gazed at her incredulously. 'Stephen is the richest man on the island, as I've already made it clear to you, and Anthea is not merely his sister, she has an income of her own, and her way of life is very different from mine. I suppose you'd call her spoiled . . . but she isn't really. It's just that she has everything.'

Laurel allowed the matter to drop, but this little sidelight did not improve her attitude towards Stephen Barrington. If his sister was such a snob that she did not think a Shannon was good enough for her – and that was what it boiled down to, of course! – then Stephen was probably ten times more of a snob, and in any case she wished she wasn't going to his house to dine tonight. But she was, and Ned was impatient to hustle her out to the car, and whether it was because he couldn't wait to see Anthea or because he was alarmed at the thought of offending his host she couldn't decide ... but she did think it was an awful pity the Barringtons had had to take over on this first night of hers on the island.

The car left the cottage and they proceeded along the bumpy road that still raised clouds of dust despite the fact it was night-time now, and the heat of the day was over. Ned explained to her, when they turned on to a much better kept road that branched off into the interior, that Stephen Barrington maintained this road because it also led to his main plantation, and Laurel thought that it was very like him to look after his own and neglect that which involved other people.

They slid smoothly along this better-kept road, between the tall shapes of trees, and eventually turned on to a private drive that wound between orderly borders of flowers and surprisingly fresh green lawns until it eventually brought them to rest before the entrance to a patio and a large Portuguese-style house. Lights streamed from the many windows of the house, spilling on to various arches and scrolled columns entwined with flowering vines, and when they had alighted and ascended the steps they found themselves in an inner patio where coloured lights were strung between the shrubs, and there was a striking impression of fairyland.

'Beautiful place, even in the dark, isn't it?' Ned commented, and Laurel agreed with him, because she couldn't very well do anything else.

Ned explained: 'We're very near to the coast of Portuguese East Africa here, and although it's a British island the atmosphere, you'll discover, is very frequently Portuguese. I believe the chap who first built this place – somewhere back in the seventeen hundreds – was a Portuguese. That's probably where Steve gets his darkness from.'

'I thought he was English. With a name like Barrington he should be.'

Ned grinned down at her.

'Oh, he's English all right, but there's more than a dash of Portuguese blood somewhere in his veins. The original founder of the place sold out to an Englishman and also married his daughter off to the new owner. That brought the Barrington name to the island. It's been British ever since.'

He had no chance to say any more, for Stephen himself came out to meet them, bending his black head in courtly greeting, and with little or nothing of the afternoon's mockery interfering with the natural gravity of his expression. Laurel nevertheless studied him with a kind of biased interest, deciding that his thick black hair was undoubtedly Portuguese, but his aquiline features were those of a buccaneer, and his piercing dark grey eyes and unusual height represented the English part of him.

He led them into the house and an impressive room where there appeared to be a lot of other people gathered, and Laurel tried hard to remember their names when she was introduced to each one of them, in order that she could place them later on. The one person she was not introduced to was her hostess, and Stephen stopped a pleasant, brown-faced young man who was just entering the room from the garden to ask:

'Have you seen Anthea, Bob?'

The young man jerked his head towards the open French window.

'When last seen she was heading in that direction,' he replied with a grin.

'Alone?'

'Of course not.'

'Brat,' Stephen said good-naturedly, and turned back to Laurel, who had been listening to the exchange with a faint curl of distaste on her lips.

'Anthea should be back fairly soon. Meanwhile, would you like a glass of sherry?'

His tone was that of the conventional host, but she gathered that he had seen the expression on her face, and was faintly amused by it. Ned declined anything to drink and wandered over to the window, from which he was able to view the starlit garden, and Laurel felt vaguely alarmed because she had been left to the tender mercies of her host. He surveyed her with a look of appreciation — her shining brown hair, slight figure in floating green chiffon and silver sandalled feet — and somewhat embarrassingly expressed his approval.

'You look very nice,' he said. 'They didn't make schoolteachers like you in my day.'

She glanced up at him with a provocative gleam in her eye.

'Ah, but that was quite a long time ago, wasn't it, Mr. Barrington?' she said.

That infuriating dark eyebrow of his jerked up.

'You have a waspish tongue, little one,' he murmured. Then he repeated his offer of a glass of sherry.

'Medium or dry?'

'Dry, please.'

He brought it to her and sat beside her on an elegant satin-covered couch. He studied her deliberately.

'You're a prickly little thing, aren't you?' he remarked. 'Are you always on the defensive, or is it that you've simply taken a dislike to me?'

'I wouldn't have the temerity to take a dislike to you, Mr. Barrington,' she replied, sipping her sherry, and peeping at him at the same time demurely.

'I thought we'd decided to drop the Mr. Barrington.' She shrugged.

'As you wish. It's not really important, is it?'

'Isn't it? I take back what I said about schoolteachers.

21

... In another few years you'll probably be more intimidating than most. Already it seems to me you have the forked tongue of a serpent.'

'You called it waspish just now,' she reminded him.

An unwilling smile chased itself across his face, and then she followed the direction of his glance as something attracted his attention, and she saw it was a young girl who had come in through the open door to the garden and, evading Ned, who would have pounced on her, made directly for her brother and the guest who had not yet been introduced to her.

'Sorry I wasn't here when you arrived,' she apologized lightly, 'but I see Steve is entertaining you.'

Laurel felt an upsurge of admiration. Anthea Barrington was as fair as her brother was dark, her long gleaming hair loose on richly tanned shoulders, her eyes sparklingly blue and alight with laughter. The dress that clothed her exquisite figure was a masterpiece of white cloudiness that must have cost a small fortune, but it was only a means of enhancing the glowing beauty of the girl herself.

Stephen looked up at her leisurely, and almost indolently.

'Hullo, brat,' he said. 'You certainly have a happy knack of absenting yourself when you know perfectly well you have duties to attend to. I haven't been presuming to entertain Miss Shannon, but at least I was on hand to welcome her this afternoon. ...' He glanced with the old mockery in his eyes at Laurel, and she felt grateful that their tête-à-tête was to end. It was difficult dealing with a man like this for any length of time, and just a little exhausting, perhaps because she had never met anyone like him before, and conversing with him was rather like taking part in mental sword-play.

'Run along, Stephen,' his sister ordered him gaily. 'You've served your purpose, but there are other people here to whom you can be just as charming – or do you have the opposite effect on some people?' with a knowledgeable gleam in her eyes. 'And I want to talk to Laurel. Ned has told me so much about her that I feel I know her already. Besides, we girls can't really have a cosy chat with a mere man hanging around!'

The mere man took his dismissal with an amiable smile in his eyes. But he warned Anthea before he departed:

'Better be careful of Laurel. She's a schoolmistress with an acid tongue, and you mustn't be deceived by the innocuous quality of her looks. They're not really innocuous at all!'

Anthea subsided beside Laurel on the settee, and the two girls exchanged a few sentences. Then Anthea produced a small gold compact from her evening bag and inspected herself in it, after which she said she thought she ought to go upstairs to her room and tidy her hair ... the night wind had blown it about, and she glanced a little mischievously across the room at Ned, who appeared to be sulking resolutely.

'Would you like to come upstairs with me?' Anthea asked. 'We can have a talk in my room.'

Laurel accompanied her hostess from the room, wondering whether the ruffled-hair incident had been a deliberate means of provoking Ned, or whether Anthea really had been engaged in some amorous incident in a corner of the garden. However, once outside in the hall she was too impressed by the house to dwell upon very much else. The hall was wide and superbly proportioned, with elegant columns supporting the ornate ceiling and a wide staircase that swept down from the upper regions like a breaking wave. Everything was on a large, lofty scale, but the evidence of wealth was tasteful and unobtrusive.

Anthea's bedroom was a revelation that took Laurel's breath away. The gleaming wood floor was strewn with valuable rugs, the dressing-table stood in a petticoat of satin, the giant built-in wardrobes had their doors standing open revealing rows and rows of dresses, and a handsome painted dressing-chest had one of its drawers pulled out to its farthest extent, and from it cascaded feminine

23

underwear.

Anthea carelessly bundled a torrent of creamy lace and chiffon back into the drawer and slammed it shut, picked up a comb from her dressing-table and sat down in front of it to deal with her hair. And over her shoulder she said to Laurel:

'It's a pretty good line you've adopted with Stephen, and as he's not used to that sort of thing it might work.'

Laurel stared at the younger girl's reflection in the mirror.

'Work?' she echoed stupidly.

Anthea swivelled round on the stool and smiled a not unkindly smile at her.

'Yes. . . . The distant attitude – the disapproval!'

'But I haven't said I disapprove of your brother!'

'No; but you do, don't you? At any rate, you don't like him!'

'I – I—'

Anthea smiled more brilliantly.

'Don't attempt to apologize,' she begged. 'It's so unusual that I find it fascinating. . . . In fact, when I first caught sight of you literally scowling at poor Steve I could hardly believe it! Ned had warned me that you're the independent type – the self-supporting type – but I never really expected anyone like you! You're so pretty, for one thing, and you must bowl a lot of men over. But Steve is the hardest man in the world to bowl over, and you could be the one to succeed where others have failed.'

It took almost a full minute for complete understanding to seep into Laurel's mind, and when it did two angry spots of colour burned in her cheeks. She snapped to her feet as if she was controlled by wires and subjected the complacently smiling Anthea to a look of cold scorn.

'If you have quite finished, Miss Barrington, I will go downstairs and join my brother,' she managed to articulate frostily. 'As for your brother. . . .' She drew in her breath and her delicate nostrils dilated slightly. 'The little I've seen of him has been enough to convince me that he's

24

utterly detestable. I do not go in for "lines", and the impression he made on me when he came to my brother's bungalow was far from favourable. In fact, I think he's the most arrogant and presumptuous man I've ever met—!'

She turned abruptly for the door, but Anthea held out a hand to her and spoke in a light and laughing voice.

'Don't be so silly! You can't be as touchy as all that! ... And all I'm suggesting is that you could have an effect on Stephen, and that in itself would be a miracle! He's so spoiled ... and women go down before him like ninepins. But you have to admit he's very handsome.'

'Is he?' Laurel demanded in an arctic tone.

Anthea surveyed her whimsically.

'Well, I think so, and I'm his sister. And I also think he's rather fascinating – and so do ninety-nine per cent of the women he meets. But you can't have it all ways, and he is rather dominating, I admit that! But that you should think him detestable strikes me as quaint.'

'There is nothing about your brother that strikes me as quaint,' Laurel replied.

Anthea rose and moved towards her.

'Have you ever been in love?' she asked.

Laurel looked startled.

'If I had I don't see why I should admit it to you,' she answered. 'But as a matter of fact, I haven't.'

'Then why don't you try falling in love with Stephen?'

'You must be joking,' Laurel said.

'Oh, indeed, I'm not.' Anthea's bright blue eyes were engagingly honest, and at the same time they gleamed with amusement. 'The idea occurred to me when I saw you for the first time downstairs ... and I still think it's the most marvellous idea I've ever had. You see, I'd rather like you for a sister-in-law, and I'm sure that Stephen finds you intriguing. Men are always bored when the same things happen to them, and when a novelty comes along it reduces their resistance. I've an idea Stephen is thinking about you at this very minute!'

25

'Nonsense!' Laurel returned.

Her hostess shrugged.

'Well, if he isn't he's wondering why I'm keeping you up here. I suppose we'd better go down.' She was obviously affected by the scarlet flags of embarrassment in Laurel's cheeks. 'I am rather a horrible brat, aren't I?' she said with a light laugh and no real sign of repentance. 'Still, I did mean it.' She touched Laurel's arm lightly as she turned to the door. 'About having you for a sister-in-law.'

'Heaven forbid!' Laurel burst out involuntarily. 'He's the last person I would want to marry, and I couldn't imagine him wanting to marry me under any circumstances.'

'Oh, you never know with Stephen,' retorted his sister, rather enigmatically.

When they reached the bottom of the wide staircase, Laurel was glad to find Ned awaiting her, to take her in to dinner, and the next part of the evening passed off quite bearably for her. On one side of her at the table was Ned and on the other a pleasant, middle-aged woman whose name she sought for frantically, until her neighbour leaned towards her with a twinkle in her eyes and whispered confidentially:

'Dalkeith.'

Laurel smiled apologetically and after that it was easy. Mrs. Dalkeith kept her occupied with reminiscences of England, while Ned chatted quite happily to another planter on his other side. Mercifully, Stephen was away down at the head of the table and Anthea kept up a lively, vivacious chatter, interspersed with the sound of appreciative male remarks. Sometimes she heard Stephen's characteristic mocking drawl and on one occasion she heard his voice become sharp and clipped in some technical discussion with a man across the table from him. Perhaps the hint of soft derision she had come to associate with him was used only when he spoke to women.

Conceited, detestable creature, she thought crossly to herself, and looked away quickly as he happened to glance up. Momentarily her gaze was caught by the sharp darkness of his, but resolutely she turned her head and concentrated her whole attention on what Mrs. Dalkeith was saying.

'Ned tells me he hasn't seen you for several years,' Mrs. Dalkeith remarked with kindly interest. 'How long do you intend to stay here now?'

It was a safe, conventional topic and Laurel was glad to be able to embark upon it.

'I really don't know yet. Ned has suggested that I live with him for as long as I want to, but I should feel altogether useless without anything to do. Pepita and the two girls manage the cottage quite easily. I can't just let poor Ned support me.'

Mrs. Dalkeith patted her hand gently. 'Whatever you feel, my dear, stay with him as long as you can. You'll be company for him. You might even be able to find something to do on the island if your conscience bothers you.'

Laurel smiled. 'I was a schoolteacher at home. I doubt whether there would be an opening of that sort on the island.'

The elder woman considered the matter thoughtfully. 'I don't know. There's no school here at all. The children all go to the boarding school on the mainland when they're old enough, or over to England. Some kind of a preparatory school here might be a good idea. I for one would be glad to send my two daughters, and you might even be able to organize something for the older ones during vacation times, not studies, but something to occupy them.' She shook her head with a whimsical grimace. 'There'll be plenty of us to greet you with open arms for doing that.' She broke off with a quick little gesture, excusing herself. 'But there I go, rushing ahead. You probably have a job or a young man in England to return to.'

Laurel shook her head. 'Neither,' she said emphatically. 'As a matter of fact, I was quite glad to give up my job. The school was a small private one and the headmistress had a sister she wanted there, in my job, but I don't think she liked to ask me outright to leave. Sometimes it was uncomfortable. I had been meaning to resign for some time, but I suppose I just stayed on through sheer obstinacy, until I found something else to go to. I didn't like being forced out. Then Ned's letter arrived.' She smiled a little shamefacedly. 'I must confess it gave me great pleasure to hand in my notice and tell them where I was going.'

Mrs. Dalkeith laughed. 'A very human satisfaction, my dear. I've often felt the same thing myself.' She glanced further along the table at a burst of laughter from around Anthea. 'Young Anthea is a lively child. The man who eventually gets her will have his hands full.'

Laurel gave a funny little twisted smile. 'Do you think any one man would be able to hold her?'

'Very easily, if he's the right one. These Barringtons fall hard when the disease eventually catches up with them.'

Laurel privately thought that the disease probably knew the uselessness of attacking where there was no heart and would not attempt to storm the fortress that was Stephen Barrington. Anthea perhaps was different. One day she might fall deeply and sincerely in love with someone – and I hope it's you, Ned dear, Laurel thought to herself, because however much she disliked Stephen, she had just realized that she could never dislike Anthea. Not entirely, at any rate.

After dinner the women went into a specially fitted room adjacent to the drawing-room to repair their make-up, while the men remained in another room with brandy and cigars. Laurel quickly repaired what make-up she wore and then caught sight of Anthea making her way across the room to her.

'I'll show you the local picture gallery while the pussies

discuss the latest gossip,' she said with a wicked glint in her eyes. 'It always helps if I'm out of the way. They can really rip me to shreds and embroider my "goings on",' she added, mimicking a high-pitched, catty voice.

A reluctant smile tugged at the corner of Laurel's mouth. 'Don't you mind?'

'Not at all,' Anthea made an airy gesture. 'I sometimes do it deliberately, to give them something to talk about.' She shook back her silky fair hair with a sideways glance at Laurel that dared her to disapprove. 'A bit of gossip keeps the old tabbies happy.'

By this time they were out in the spacious hall with its lofty pillars and Laurel threw her companion a curious glance.

'What about the ... the partners ... who aid you in supplying items for the local gossip column?' she inquired tentatively.

Anthea shrugged. 'They know what to expect from me.' Momentarily a touch of grimness set her soft mouth. 'If any of them take me seriously, it's their own fault.' The next moment the seriousness was gone in the usual gay event of laughter and chatter.

Laurel followed her more slowly as they reached the wide staircase, thinking of Ned, who even though he had known what she was, had not been able to escape being hurt.

'By the way,' Anthea said, as they reached the top of the stairs, 'do you ride?'

'I used to, when we lived in the country, but I haven't done so for ages.'

'Doesn't matter,' Anthea answered with gay carelessness. 'You'll soon pick it up again. Ned hasn't any horses, but we have plenty here.'

'You seem well acquainted with my brother's affairs,' Laurel commented dryly.

'Oh, everybody knows everybody else's business on the island,' Anthea answered with typical airy inconsequence. By this time she was leading the way along a corridor and she flashed a glance at the other girl over her shoulder. 'Stephen is the one who really amazes me, though. He gets to know the most odd things, especially those you would rather he didn't,' she added with a rueful laugh.

Stephen would, Laurel decided with a touch of acidity in her thoughts. In fact, Stephen had things far too much his own way.

Anthea found a switch and the long gallery immediately became flooded with light. A slim white hand that had never done a day's work in its owner's life waved gaily at the portrait they stood in front of.

'Meet Miguel Felipe Luis Castelanho de Valente, the founder of Castelanto.'

Laurel looked up at the portrait interestedly. Yes, there was the same thick black hair, springing off a tanned forehead in exactly the same way that Stephen's did, but the rest of the face was distinctly Portuguese and the man was far shorter than his distant descendant.

Dom Miguel's wife was a rather plain Portuguese woman, but their daughter was beautiful. There was also a son, dark and good-looking – with a mischievous tilt to his mouth that somehow vaguely reminded Laurel of the girl at her side, in spite of Anthea's fairness. The next portrait in line was that of a rather pompous Englishman.

'Jonathan Barrington,' Anthea said. 'I believe he was a bit of a nitwit. He looks it, anyway. He married old Dom Miguel's daughter. I don't know what she saw in him. It was probably parental pressure. The son moved out and a bit later he was appointed governor of one of the other Portuguese islands nearby. Lord, I sound like a walking guide book!' she laughed. 'Anyway, you'll probably meet one of his descendants before long. Manoel drops in on us every now and again.'

Laurel was about to pursue the subject of the unknown Manoel, fearing that Stephen's name was about to crop up again, but Anthea moved on to the next portrait and stopped there with a delighted smile on her piquant features.

'My favourite ancestor,' she said with a chuckle of pure glee, and leaned forward to switch on an additional light over the portrait, throwing into sharp clarity all the audacious buccaneering attraction of the painted figure. It was only too clear whom he resembled, even though Nicholas Barrington had possessed hair of a vivid and flaming red.

'Nicholas Barrington, the buccaneer,' Anthea said, savouring the words deliciously. 'He kidnapped his bride from an adjoining island and when they came to rescue her they couldn't prise her loose from him with a ton of dynamite. She wasn't having any. She'd been kidnapped and she was very definitely staying kidnapped.' She spread out her arms and sighed with pure envy. 'Wouldn't it be wonderful to be loved like that?'

'I don't think so,' Laurel disagreed. 'Suppose she had hated the sight of the man she was forced to marry?'

Anthea gave her a roguish glance and pointed to the portrait. 'You tell me just one thing a hundred per cent truthfully, Miss Laurel Shannon – if that man carried you off and forced you to marry him, would you be able to hate him?'

Laurel glanced up at the portrait again and smiled very slightly, shaking her head. The admission was made with extreme reluctance, even though there was just enough difference from the present-day Stephen Barrington to allow her to make it without feeling self-conscious. Nicholas Barrington was laughing and audacious, instead of mocking and derisive. His eyes were a bright, challenging blue instead of a too perceptive grey. For the rest, though, the tall strong body, the thin tapering hands, the arrogant poise of the head, even the features – it was Stephen and nobody else.

Anthea leaned forward and switched off the portrait light. 'I suppose we'd better go back now. I'll show you the rest some other time. I always think the others come as an anti-climax, though, except Stephen himself, but then I'm prejudiced,' she added, with a side glance that Laurel did not quite catch. 'On second thoughts though, there is somebody else worth having a look at.' She went further along the gallery and again switched on one of the portrait lights. 'Lavinia Barrington.'

This time the portrait was of a tall young woman of striking beauty. She had been painted in a severe black gown, but her stance suggested that she should have been wearing male attire and wielding a sword. Here at last were eyes of a dark, piercing grey, lit with a mocking light that was too familiar.

'One of these days I'll lend you the family history to read about her,' Anthea offered. 'She was a holy terror with a sword. The family apparently turned up another pompous idiot like old Jonathan at that time and she was the bane of his life. He was her brother, by the way,' she added gratuitously. 'He did his best to marry her off, but she wasn't having any. In the end she received a fatal wound while still young, defending the palace against pirates.'

'Perhaps she preferred it that way,' Laurel said quietly. 'She looks ... rather independent, and they didn't care for feminine independence in those days.'

Anthea gave the portrait a rather curious glance, as if she had never thought of that aspect of it before.

'No, I suppose they didn't,' she said, and leaned forward to switch off the light.

They returned to the staircase, Laurel with her thoughts still in the past, thinking of the girl who had preferred to live a life that had brought her to a violent death rather than be forced to marry someone she had perhaps despised. It had been in every line of her young body; the pride and the desire for freedom. Somehow she had escaped the conventional restricted upbringing of her time and she had never been able to fit into it later. Probably she really had preferred to end her life that way.

Suddenly she stiffened, because she realized that Stephen had come out of the drawing-room and was standing at the foot of the staircase, watching them descend. She attempted to keep her gaze steadily in front of her, but all the time she was over-conscious of his probing eyes watching them both, one a vivid tropical flower and the other a pale, cool nymph; then his glance went to his sister with the amused, tolerant affection he seemed to keep specially for her.

'I thought you'd gone out into the garden again. It seems that I misjudged you.'

Anthea gave him a mock reproachful glance. 'And I was taking a very solemn tour of the picture gallery with Teacher!'

Laurel, remembering some of the other girl's comments, could hardly agree that it had been solemn.

'No lectures from Miss Schoolteacher?' Stephen inquired, slanting a half taunting glance at Laurel.

'I was lecturing her instead,' Anthea replied wickedly. 'She knows all about our family skeletons now.'

'All of them?' Laurel felt the derisive glance slide over her. 'No wonder she came downstairs blushing.' Again that speculative rather unkind glance that mocked at her youth. 'But then even teachers have to learn.'

'I might point out that I finished training some time ago,' Laurel stated evenly, deliberately choosing to misunderstand him. 'I've been teaching myself for nearly a year.'

'You still have a vast amount to learn, my child.'

'He means about men,' Anthea chimed in shamelessly. She gave Laurel an interested glance. 'I must get you aside one day and give you some instruction on the subject.'

'She needs to learn that from a man.'

'I don't think I care to learn from anyone, thank you,' Laurel interrupted firmly. Much as she had decided she like Anthea, she could have slapped her at that moment. As for Stephen, her fingers literally ached to strike his dark face.

Anthea ignored the remark and subjected her brother to an inquiring scrutiny.

'Are you offering yourself as a teacher?'

'And be accused of cradle-snatching?'

Laurel clenched her hands at her sides. In just one moment, she thought wildly, she would lose complete control of herself. What would he do if she did hit him? It was hard to predict with a man so unaccountable and enigmatic as Stephen Barrington. Retaliation would be something unpleasant, though. She could at least count on that.

She swung on her heel, paused to look back at them. 'I'll leave you alone to your discussion. I'm afraid it's beginning to bore me.' And that, she thought, continuing her journey to the door of the drawing-room, should successfully blot her copybook with the Barringtons, which conclusion, since she had come with the deliberate intention of making herself so disagreeable that neither Barrington would have the least desire to invite her there again, pleased her immensely.

She had just reached the door of the drawing-room, when she heard Stephen say behind her:

'Run along, Anthea. I want to dance with Laurel.'

She heard the sound of Anthea's high heels tapping off, then quick, firm footsteps followed her and when she turned Stephen was so close behind her that she involuntarily recoiled, but almost instantly her slender figure bristled with defiance and indignation.

'I have no wish to dance with you.'

'That's just too bad.' His voice was unsympathetic and his fingers on her arm had the feel of steel clamps. Whether she liked it or not, she found herself somehow inside the lovely room that had been deprived of its rugs to permit them to dance on the polished boards, held closely in his arms. He danced well, with assurance and a certain lithe grace, but she was annoyed to find that he was making her dance exceedingly well also, when she had been quite sure that their steps could not possibly match. She was also aggrieved to find that his nearness was having an oddly disturbing effect on her.

'What are you trembling for?' Stephen asked calmly. 'Haven't you ever danced with a man before?'

'Of course I have.' She knew that a betraying colour had risen in her cheeks, but his words had satisfactorily banished that queer breathlessness. 'I expect it's just the effect of dancing with you,' she added sarcastically. 'You have such a devastating personality it completely overwhelms me.'

'I'm honoured,' Stephen replied with the derisive thread so clear in his voice that her fingers tightened momentarily on his shoulder. The familiar glance she hated rested on her fingers in their impotent gesture of defiance and dislike. 'My personality again?' he murmured sardonically. 'I had no idea it was so upsetting.'

Laurel pressed her lips together hard and forbore to make any reply.

'What's the matter?' he jeered. 'Can't you think of anything particularly flaying to spit at me?'

It seemed impossible to her that she could so intensely dislike anyone in such a short period of time. Again and again she had to remind herself that they had met for the first time only that afternoon, but it already seemed a lifetime that she had been subjected to his taunts, a lifetime ago when she had first heard that mocking, derisive voice. What was it Beryl Cornish had said about him – 'Stephen never leaves you long in doubt as to how you feel about him.' Whatever else, he was a man a girl could never be indifferent to.

The music of the record-player stopped suddenly and she found herself directly in front of one of the open french windows that led into the garden. Without stopping to think, she freed herself determinedly as his hold slackened at the end of the dance, and took the couple of steps that brought her out on to the terrace, but her escape was shortlived.

'Yes, it is a little warm inside,' Stephen's voice agreed

equably from behind her and she felt his fingers, firm and hard, beneath her elbow, assisting her down the steps into the moonlit gardens with their festoons of coloured lights. 'You'd better take a little walk to cool off,' he added, releasing her as they reached the pathway below.

'I don't wish to take a walk.'

Yet, nevertheless, she started to walk rather quickly away from him, not caring in which direction she went, but quite conscious that he was following her at a leisurely pace. The result was that she caught the floating chiffon of her dress on a bush and had to stand and fumble with it, finding that anger had made her fingers too clumsy, while he caught up with her. Then of course she had to suffer the final indignity of having him release her with calm, sure fingers.

This time he caught her arm and held on to it. 'Come here, and don't act so much like a scared rabbit. I'm not going to follow out Anthea's instructions.' The dark eyes were narrowed, watching her with a hint of gentle teasing instead of mockery, but she was beyond being beguiled by any such overture of friendship, especially when he tilted up her head to watch her expression closely, with that tiny half smile playing around his firm mouth. 'It's a pity that you're not a few years older, or I might be tempted.'

Laurel jerked herself free. 'I'm quite conscious of the honour,' she retorted scathingly, 'but I'm afraid I can't oblige you. Wouldn't I do as I am now?' That sounded dangerous and she added hastily, 'In any event, the prospect doesn't appeal to me in the least.'

'It's just as well,' he retorted coolly. 'I like my women experienced.'

That was the final straw. She raised her hand in blind fury, only to find it caught in ruthless fingers that arrested its motion, while his other arm clipped her around the waist with cruel strength. In the moonlight and the glow of the little coloured lights she saw that the expression on his face was not pleasant.

36

'You've been like a piece of poisonous ivy all evening. What's the matter with you?'

Laurel attempted to jerk free, but found it quite impossible, and privately she was a little aghast, because she had never imagined a man's strength could be quite so overpowering.

'I don't have to explain myself to you.'

'No, you don't, my child – but since I can't fathom out what all this is about, anyway, perhaps I'd better give you reason for really disliking me,' he retorted harshly.

The arm around her waist tightened and the hand that grasped her wrist released its hold, fastened instead into the clustered curls at the back of her head.

Laurel went deathly white in the moonlight, but she nevertheless met the unpleasant glint in his eyes with defiant bravery.

'What is this – lesson number one?'

'Call it what you like,' he said, and kissed her.

She had been kissed before, casual meaningless kisses that she had endured tolerantly after a dance, but never like this; never a kiss that was meant to be a punishment, that bruised her lips and shattered her fury and left her feeling small and bewildered. It gave her no chance to soften to him or to respond, even had she desired to do so. It was the kiss of an experienced man who meant to hurt and who succeeded.

'Put that under the heading of experience,' he said as he released her.

'I will.' She raised a shaky hand to her bruised lips. 'Under the sub-heading of unpleasant!'

'Don't deceive yourself, my child. The way you've been acting tonight, you deserve far more.' He turned her towards the house, drawing her along with him back to the brilliantly lighted windows, as if his one desire now was to be rid of her. 'And now I gather you would like to shake the dust of this iniquitous household off your dainty silver shoes,' he finished sarcastically.

'If I didn't want to wear them again, I would burn

them,' she snapped back childishly.

She did not know or care what excuse he made to Ned, but she was wholeheartedly thankful to see her brother coming over to the chair where Stephen had deposited her on returning to the drawing-room. Her head was swimming with the shards of her fury and her bruised lips still throbbed from that ruthless kiss.

Ned looked down at her anxiously. 'Are you feeling all right, pet?'

Laurel smiled wanly at the old childish name. 'Just a bit dizzy. I expect it's the heat in here.'

'Steve said you wanted me. Would you like to go home?'

Laurel hesitated a moment, then nodded. 'You could come back here after you drop me.'

Ned shook his head. 'I think I've had about enough as well.' He grinned ruefully. 'Must be getting old. I can't take the fleshpots like I used to.'

'Can't stand the sight of Anthea Barrington flirting with other men,' Laurel amended grimly to herself, and wished she had never heard the name Barrington.

'I'll get my wrap,' she said aloud, and stood up.

As she made her way to the blessedly deserted room where she had left her wrap, she felt suddenly and overwhelmingly tired. It seemed as if her body was one aching bruise from the relentless grip of Stephen's hands. It only needed the sight of Anthea flitting past the doorway, her laughter as light and gay as a tropical breeze, to set the final seal on her longing to get away from this spreading, beautiful house with its suggestion of restrained wealth and its mocking, hateful owner.

CHAPTER TWO

LAUREL awoke late on the morning following her arrival on the island. The headache she had pretended to have the night before had become splitting reality and when Pepita entered her room with a daintily laid tray she decided then and there that eating was the last thing she could manage.

Even so, the fragrant smell of freshly made coffee was tempting and she wrinkled her nose appreciatively.

'That smells good, Pepita.'

The woman set the tray carefully down on her knees, her dark face creased in a smile.

'That is good, miss,' she said in her prim, stilted English and, bobbing her queer little curtsey, went out of the room, leaving Laurel to stare at small twisted rolls, fresh yellow butter and ripe delicious fruit and decide that she did feel just a little hungry after all.

It was an unusual luxury for her to breakfast in bed and not something she intended to continue, but this morning it had a luxurious appeal she did not resist, so that the depression and weariness, the lingering lassitude that had gripped her limbs, slowly disappeared, taking with them the headache that had threatened to spoil her day. She felt a return of the happy excitement of yesterday morning, before a man with mocking grey eyes had come into her life and spoilt everything with the horrid, taunting derision underlying the soft tones of his voice.

Drat Stephen Barrington, she told herself firmly, and slid the covers back to stand barefooted on the soft carpet. He was not going to be allowed to spoil her holiday. There was no reason why she should even think of him, although on the other hand there was no hope whatsoever of pretending he did not exist. He was simply not the type of man a woman could forget, whether she thought

39

of him with liking or with complete distaste.

She padded over to the window on her small bare feet, then drew back quickly to reach for her dressing-gown in case anyone should be standing below. Even though she smiled at the thought, she still wrapped herself in the conventional dark blue garment that had served her well for so many years, then she went back to the window, drawing in the soft scents of the clustered tropical flowers outside, delighting in the unfamiliar sight of feathery palm fronds against a brilliant sky and the flutter of a jewel-bright wing from the direction of the gum trees with their red blossoms adding yet another touch of colour to the already fantastically beautiful scene.

Because it was all too rich and vivid to take in at once, she sent her thoughts back to what her days had been only a short time ago; the single room apartment that had been her home since both mother and father had died in the fatal rail accident. She had not been unhappy in that prettily furnished little room and old Mrs. Grunsted, the landlady, had been a friendly and helpful woman. Sometimes she would take care of pretty little Maureen Jordon, while the elder woman's daughter and son-in-law would take the landlady out for the evening, and sometimes when Laurel came home cold and dripping wet on a winter evening, she would find herself led firmly into the kitchen, where a hot meal awaited her.

And then there was the school. She had gone there herself in her childhood, passing from pupil to pupil teacher, giving up almost every evening to study while she went through training school, her only relaxation the curious fascination for classical Greek dancing that she was able to indulge at the Physical Culture Institute a short distance from where she studied. Then there had been the tensed expectancy and the apprehension of the final examinations, the moment of triumph when the heavily sealed document was placed in her hands and she had taken up her position as kindergarten teacher in the local school where she herself had once been a pupil. Only a short time afterwards had come the chance of a job at the private school where she had worked until she left to come to Ladrana and in the beginning it had been everything she had hoped for, until the little jealousies and intrigues had crept in.

But that was all in the past, and she shrugged off the unwelcome thought of those last few months as she turned from the window and went to investigate the possibilities of a bath. After all, she had always meant to leave, intending to go back to studying for a while, so that she could pass on to a higher grade of teaching, but the exquisite motions of the dancing she had taken up had demanded more and more of her time, so she had put off the actual moment of giving it up to go back to intensive study in the evenings.

Then had come this momentous upheaval, the unexpected change that had resulted in her being here in beautiful, tropical Ladrana. She could not yet accustom herself to having plenty of time on her hands, nor to the thought that there was now no need to rise almost with the crack of dawn; and above all it was wonderful not to have to combat the petty little intrigues that had made life at the school so uncomfortable the last few months. Of course there were a few little unwelcome items in her life even now – such as Stephen Barrington.

No, she told herself firmly. He should not intrude into her thoughts again, even though it was rather comical and absurd and brought a smile to her lips to label him as an 'item'.

Pepita came into sight climbing the narrow stairway as Laurel, wandering along the passage, was starting to wonder if the place really did have a bathroom.

'The water it has been poured for the bath,' Pepita said, somewhat to Laurel's relief, even though she had known at the back of her mind that Ned must have made arrangements of some kind.

The bathroom turned out to be a small outhouse where water was boiled in a large tank and tipped into a sunken bath that had been carved out of rock and lined with tiles. A large mirror was fitted up over a neatly made cupboard that looked as if it was Ned's handiwork, and on a small shelf to one side of the mirror a large jar of highly scented bath crystals and perfumed talc made her smile affectionately at Ned's forethought. The tiles around the bath also looked new. He had probably fitted them specially for her, being content himself with a plain rock bath.

Pepita inquired if she needed assistance, but at Laurel's refusal slipped discreetly out of the room. Smiling to herself, Laurel tipped a handful of Ned's gift down into the warm water of the bath and lowered herself into it.

Once a brightly coloured bird came and perched himself upon the windowsill, high up in the room where no human eyes could peer in, but, her thoughts wandering again, it was not until Ned's voice sounded outside that she realized how long she had been in the bathhouse.

'Hey, are you still in there?' he called out unceremoniously, and Laurel guiltily climbed out of the bath.

'Won't be a moment,' she called, and hastily towelled herself dry and pulled on the white linen slacks and blouse she had brought with her.

Ned grinned when she appeared. 'I thought you'd fallen down the plughole,' he commented.

That reminded her that the water was still in the bath and she turned back quickly to pull out the plug and watch the water gurgle away through the tunnel that had been cut in the living rock.

'How do you like our ultra-mod cons?' Ned inquired, watching her intrigued expression. 'Rather ingenious, eh, what?' he added with an atrociously affected accent.

'Idiot!' Laurel retorted with a quick smile up at him.

'Thank you, my dear sister,' Ned said with a bow. 'Thank you very much.' He dropped his bantering tone and added, 'I'm going into town. Coming?'

She nodded eagerly, then gestured towards her informal clothes. 'Had I better change?'

Ned shook his head carelessly. 'You're all right as you are. Nobody bothers to dress up much in Milton.'

He waited while she took the remainder of her belongings from the bathroom back into the house and a few minutes later she joined him at the car, the faintest suggestion of make-up accentuating her piquant features. The burnished hair, although still damp, was already beginning to cluster into its short, natural curls. She looked more like an excited pixie than a schoolteacher, especially with her blue-green eyes glowing with anticipation.

Ned whistled softly and shook his head. 'Heaven help Laurana!'

Laurel flushed. 'Stop it, Ned. I know I'm not in the least pretty.'

'Go tell it to the Marines,' Ned retorted inelegantly, and started up the car.

The usual infiltration of dust crept in through the window almost immediately, but Laurel, although she noticed it, was more concerned with watching the unfamiliar and colourful scenery than in wasting time dwelling on any slight discomfort.

The little native settlement was just as it had been the day before, almost as if time itself had stood still in the interval. Naked piccanins still played in the dust and some still ignored the car while others turned to stand wide-eyed until it was out of sight.

'How did you enjoy the party last night – at least until you acquired your headache?' Ned asked, without taking his eyes off the winding, bumpy road.

'Very nice,' Laurel replied, but something in her tone must have given her away.

Ned glanced sideways at her. 'Taken a dislike to someone?'

Dislike! At the very thought of Stephen Barrington her eyes sparkled dangerously. How could a mild word like 'dislike' describe what she felt for that odious creature?

43

'I don't think I care very much for your friend Stephen,' she said guardedly.

'You don't like Steve?' Ned sounded positively astonished. 'There's nothing about him to dislike.'

'Oh, isn't there!'

She could have named quite a few traits she found far from likeable, including taking advantage of his masculine strength to punish her because she had not fallen a victim to his mocking charm like everyone else.

'You'll probably change your mind when you get to know him better,' Ned said easily, apparently not in the least perturbed.

'I don't think I want to know him. He's about everything I dislike in a man and far too fond of having his own way.'

She was a little sorry after the words left her lips, because she did not want Ned to get the idea that she was going to dislike or find fault with his friends, but at least it would serve to let him know that she had no particular desire to become closely acquainted with Stephen Barrington and, knowing her wishes, her brother might tactfully keep off the subject and not accept any invitations on her behalf – not that she was likely to receive any, considering the way in which she had parted from Stephen last night.

She glanced at Ned sideways to see how he was taking it, but he still looked quite undisturbed and was even grinning to himself in a way she could not understand.

They turned on to the smooth road that led to Milton and for a while the conversation concerned her old life back in the small Kentish town she had left to come to Ladrana, then at last the first few buildings of Milton straggled into sight, a motley collection that were mainly English colonial style, interspersed with a sprinkling of the distinctly Spanish or Portuguese type dwellings that seemed far more appropriate to the island.

'You'll find the people a bit of a mixture,' Ned said with a nod towards a knot of people talking together and gesticulating excitedly outside one of the houses. 'It's been British for quite a time, but the island was originally settled by the Portuguese.' He gestured towards the unseen sea. 'The nearest island out there is Portuguese too. I'll make arrangements for you to visit it some time. They're a friendly crowd.'

The buildings were getting closer together now, a curious mixture of old and new, until they at last reached the centre of the town, with its wide streets and beautifully set out gardens. Ned drove around for a while, pointing out various landmarks, the fountains in the gardens that were always illuminated at festival times – unfortunately reminding Laurel too vividly of the illuminated fountain in Stephen's gardens – the modern public buildings and business houses of the town and the harbour where an assortment of vessels were anchored. In the deeper part she saw the coastal freighter that had brought her to Ladrana still unloading its cargo, a flurry of brown figures on its decks. A slim white yacht rode the slight swell gracefully a short distance along, with a miscellany of native craft – and then the droning of a powerful engine crept faintly into the scented air.

'That sounds like Steve,' Ned remarked, and nodded as a slim dart of a vessel rounded the headland in a plume of angry wash and spray, the fiendish howling of its engine a song of power and arrogance.

Just the sort of craft he would own, Laurel thought scornfully. It was easy to imagine that dark, buccaneer face intent and at the same time assured, the strong, ruthless hands gripping the wheel of the powerful craft, battling the force of its throbbing engines as the vessel turned in a sweeping arc and reduced speed, its needle nose lowering to meet the water again, the song of power dying to a muted thrumming and at last dying away altogether.

Reluctantly, she followed Ned down to the quay, watching as a tall white-clad figure jumped lightly from the moored boat and turned to them with a half laconical gesture of one hand in greeting.

45

' 'Morning, Ned.' The mocking eyes with their too astute knowledge slid from the man to the taut figure of the girl at his side. 'How's the headache, Laurel?'

'Quite gone, thank you,' Laurel replied stiffly, resisting the impulse to say that the headache had just arrived.

One dark brow jerked upwards quizzically. 'I'm glad to hear it.'

He knew quite well that she had never had a headache, since it had been his invention in the first place. The knowledge made her hands clench at her sides in the helpless fury she was coming to associate with his presence.

'I've just been showing Laurel around the town,' Ned put in. 'We were just about to retire for a cool drink. Care to join us?'

To Laurel's immense relief, she saw Stephen shake his dark head. ' 'Fraid I can't make it. I've just been up coast and I have to get straight along to the warehouse.' There was a glint of amusement in his eyes as they went to the girl. 'Anthea has been muttering all the morning about having you over to lunch if you're free. She's probably gone out to your place now.' His glance went back to Ned. 'Why don't you both come along?'

Ned hesitated, then shook his head. 'Thanks, Steve, but I'd better not. I meant to have a look at the sisal this afternoon and I don't think I should put it off any longer.' He turned to where Laurel, at his side, was anticipating and dreading his next words. 'There's no reason why you shouldn't go, though.'

There was every reason, Laurel thought furiously. Ned knew very well that she did not like Stephen Barrington, yet he was calmly proposing to abandon her to an afternoon with the said Stephen Barrington. It could not be ignorance of the true state of her feelings, because she had made that clear enough, and on glancing at her brother she detected a rather bland look on his face and guessed what it meant.

So Ned thought her dislike would abate on closer acquaintance? As if that could ever happen – however long she knew him!

She shrugged, rather ungraciously it must be admitted, and Stephen seemed to take the matter as settled.

'I'll pick you up a bit later, then.'

Laurel parted her lips mutinously, to state that she had no desire whatsoever to lunch at Castelanto and that she would far rather look at the sisal with Ned, but she reluctantly closed them upon the unspoken words.

She listened to Ned deciding where they would go, heard him arrange for Stephen to pick her up later, all the time with her helpless annoyance seething inside her, but she made no move to demur. She did vow to herself, though, that in future she would have some excuse ready to explain why she could not go. At the moment both of them knew it was too soon for her to have received invitations from anybody else on the island.

Ned led her into what looked to be a private garden, but just as she started to wonder rather anxiously whether he had made a mistake and they were trespassing, a waiter came out to take their order. Sitting back in the shade of a blue-flowered jacaranda and sipping a cool drink appreciatively, she found some of her anger abating, but she still regarded the forthcoming afternoon with no degree of pleasure and a vast amount of reluctance.

Stephen joined them only a short time later and they moved outside, to where a powerful dark maroon car was parked. Laurel's glance went over it with admiration, but at the same time dislike, because of its owner. By no stretch of imagination could she see dust entering this car, even on the worst road.

Ned gave her a grin. 'See you later,' he said with not too well hidden complacency, and went off down the road with his loping stride, leaving Laurel annoyed with him but also confused and conscious of a stupid sense of panic that made her want to call him back. Unconsciously she

47

even made some slight move towards him, until she heard Stephen's slow, drawling voice behind her.

'The car is in this direction.'

She turned, with a tensed acceptance of the inevitable, and slid into the seat, avoiding touching him as he held open the door. When he slammed it shut and went round the front of the car to his own side she unobtrusively inched as far as possible away from the place where he would be sitting.

Before starting the car he turned in the seat to glance down at her. 'Stop acting so much like a sulky child. I'll keep out of the way all the afternoon if you like. You didn't hate Anthea on sight, did you?'

Without waiting for her reply, he turned his attention back to the car and started the engine, but as no answer seemed to be forthcoming after a few minutes, he remarked a little grimly:

'I'm still waiting for a reply.'

Laurel flashed him a startled glance. 'Oh no. . . .' She broke off and continued more slowly. 'No, I don't hate Anthea. I rather like her, in fact.'

'Good.'

She did not know quite what to make of the monosyllabic reply and a quick glance at his face only disclosed that his expression was completely unreadable.

'What would you have done if I had said yes?' she asked curiously, surprised at herself the next moment when she heard her voice asking the question.

'Taken you back to Ned's place and left you there.'

'Oh!' She digested that in silence for a while, realizing suddenly and incomprehensibly in that moment that he cared as much for his sister as she did for Ned and trying to decide where it fitted into her once well integrated picture of him.

A half glance at him showed that he was grinning rather maliciously 'What's the matter?' His jibing voice had a too complete perception. 'Doesn't it fit in?' A slanting glance of the same unkind amusement slid over her.

'Think about it for a while, teacher. You have a lot to learn yet.'

Laurel flashed him a mutinous look and bit back the retort that was on her tongue, sure that it would only have called forth more of the biting derision had she pointed out that she had no desire whatsoever to learn if it involved him.

For quite a time she fell into a glowering silence, longing to somehow carry the fire into the enemy camp, but not daring to. Under her dislike she was just a little afraid of him. There was a too clear memory of last night. Even though he might deride her youth and inexperience, he would not hesitate to use his own experience and worldly cynicism as a weapon to punish her if any of her seemingly ineffectual darts turned out to have sharp points after all and stung their way through his insufferable assurance.

A slight movement from Stephen broke into her thoughts and she glanced at him sideways, to see one hand holding out the slim gold cigarette case.

'Cigarette?'

'No, thank you.'

In her own ears her voice sounded very prim and reserved and she half expected him to comment on it, but either he did not notice or had lost interest in baiting her for the moment.

'Light one for me.'

He carelessly tipped the cigarette case, with its built-in lighter, into her lap, and Laurel instantly felt the resentful antagonism rising in her. Did he think every woman was just dying to fall in with his careless orders? Almost at the same time she saw the very faintest suspicion of a grin on his dark face and realized that he was expecting her to refuse – so of course she did not.

With fingers that trembled slightly, she drew a cigarette out of the case, lit it silently and handed it to him. He took it between thin, strong fingers, glancing down, and she flashed him a resentful glance.

'There's no lipstick on it, if that's what you're looking for. I use a brand that doesn't come off.'

'I know,' he said calmly. 'I wouldn't have asked you to light it otherwise.'

She could have bitten out her tongue the moment she had spoken, but it was by far too late.

'And if you think I'm going to apologize for last night,' he continued, still in that bland, faintly derisive voice, 'I haven't the slightest intention of doing so. You deserved everything you got.'

'Sometimes, Stephen,' she said very clearly and deliberately, 'I feel like hitting you – hard!'

'You know what happens to little girls who do that,' he drawled tauntingly.

Laurel clenched her hands at her sides in swift, impotent fury and for one wild moment actually wished she was back in England, where there was no aggravating and thoroughly detestable Stephen Barrington.

At last they swung into the private road, through the high ornate gates and into the gardens of Castelanto, to stop in the tiled patio. Anthea was waiting for them on the terrace, surrounded, it seemed to Laurel, by cats. At first sight there seemed to be dozens of them, then she noticed that the family comprised two full-grown Siamese and four kittens, with the distinctive markings just beginning to show in their creamy fur.

'Have you got that menagerie out again?' Stephen commented tolerantly, and did not seem in the least surprised when one of the cats took a fantastic flying leap at him and landed on his shoulder. He hooked it down with one hand, scratched it under the chin with a grin and replaced it on the floor, where it wound itself around his legs, purring loudly.

'Meet Princess Flower of White Jade,' Anthea introduced. 'We just call her Princess, though – and that's Prince Meng looking aloof over there.'

Prince Meng stalked proudly over to Laurel and condescended to allow her to tickle him behind his sharp pointed ears.

'By the way, Steve,' Anthea said, as Laurel straightened up, 'Peter Marshall is here. He wants to see you about the southern plantation.'

Stephen nodded, detaching himself from Princess. 'Keep Laurel amused.' His grin jeered at her. 'She might miss me.'

Before Laurel could think of something appropriately scathing to say, he was gone, and Anthea, with a light chuckle of laughter, led the way into the house, leaving the Siamese in sole possession of the terrace.

'Don't let him annoy you,' she warned. 'He will do it all the more if he thinks he's getting under your skin.'

Laurel shrugged. 'I hardly think he's likely to do that,' she replied with an assumption of indifference.

'Nevertheless, my pet,' Anthea stated calmly, 'he is. Furthermore,' the amazing Miss Barrington added, 'within a week you'll be in love with him and, because I thoroughly approve of the idea, I shall see that he marries you.'

For a moment Laurel looked both shocked and angry, then the absurd humour of the situation struck her and she burst into quite irresistible laughter.

'Anthea, you're quite mad!'

'Oh, naturally,' Anthea agreed blandly. 'But I usually get my own way.'

'Perhaps you do, but this is one instance where you're going to be bitterly disappointed,' Laurel stated with great determination.

'Oh, I don't know.' Anthea put her head on one side, considering the matter. 'You're going about things the right way, of course. Stephen is definitely interested. It's quite unusual for a woman to pretend to dislike him on sight.'

'Will you please get it into your head that I'm not pretending?' Laurel retorted sharply, as her amusement gave way to exasperation. 'I hate to say it, as he's your brother, but I genuinely think he's the most detestable person I've ever had the misfortune to meet, and I should be quite happy never to see him again. As for this "interest" on his part, it's merely his way of deriding everybody who doesn't happen to be lucky enough to be Stephen Barrington.'

'A week,' Anthea said complacently. 'I'll give you just a week.'

'Shall we talk of something else?' Laurel suggested firmly.

Anthea shook her head sadly. 'You're hopeless!'

Laurel followed the girl along a corridor and out on to another part of the terrace, forbearing to make any reply, because Anthea was sure to cap it with some audacious statement.

On this part of the terrace comfortable wicker chairs and little glass-topped tables were set out on the sun-warmed stone, but with a little shock Laurel realized that this terrace must be part of the one she had been on last night, the one that opened out from the drawing-room – because further along, in the garden below, was a path she recognized.

'I think we'll have a cold drink,' Anthea announced, ringing a tiny bell on one of the tables, and Laurel was glad of the interruption to break the trend her thoughts had been taking.

A slim, dark maid came out on to the terrace in reply to Anthea's ring and went away again with a flutter of a full, bright skirt when Anthea had given her instructions about what they wanted.

'It's lovely, isn't it?' Anthea was leaning against the balcony, looking down into the gardens. 'I don't think I ever want to leave Castelanto or even Ladrana.'

Laurel turned curiously to look at her. 'What about when you get married?'

Anthea shrugged. 'That's a long way off. Perhaps I don't have it in me to fall permanently in love,' she added with a curious little twist to her lips, and, because she was thinking of Ned, Laurel let the matter drop.

Men's voices sounded from the room behind them and Laurel felt herself tensing instinctively, but when he came out on to the terrace Stephen was not alone. The man with him was dark-haired and good-looking, but although he was only a few inches shorter than the man at his side he looked somehow only of medium height.

Laurel found herself looking into brown eyes that held an expression of such bold admiration she knew a flush must be rising to her face, and the faintly sardonic grin on Stephen's face did not improve matters. She was quite unaware that Anthea was frowning as Stephen performed the introduction, because she was still too conscious of the intent regard of the man who managed one of the Barrington plantations.

'How long are you over here for, Miss Shannon?' Peter Marshall asked, holding on to her hand longer than was strictly necessary, so that Laurel had to tug it free, again over-conscious of the grin on Stephen's face that mocked at her discomfort under the intent, admiring stare.

'I don't know yet,' she answered. 'I'm only here for a holiday. I have a career to return to in England.'

'She teaches school,' Stephen murmured informatively, and Laurel knew instinctively what was coming. The joke was even beginning to pall a little.

'A schoolteacher?'

Laurel looked up at the young man somewhat defiantly. 'Why not?'

'You don't look like a schoolteacher,' he countered, as if that was an irrefutable argument. 'You're too young, and you look more like a pupil yourself.'

'There are plenty of things she still has to learn,' Stephen's drawl agreed from the background.

Laurel took a firm grip on herself and would not look round at him. Instead she followed Anthea's example and sat down sedately on one of the wicker chairs, scooping up a Siamese kitten that had wandered around from the other part of the terrace. With the little animal curled up in her lap and purring she had an excuse for her attention to be wholly taken up whenever she felt it necessary.

The young maid came out with the drinks Anthea had ordered and then was sent away again to get drinks for the men. Stephen took up a stance, leaning against the balustrade, that enabled him to watch all of them, but Peter took a chair opposite Laurel, shaking his head with a faint, disbelieving smile.

'Did you really teach school in England?'

'Of course I did.' She smiled because, after all, his amazement was nothing at all like Stephen's mocking jeers. 'It was only a small school, though. In the larger ones the teachers are usually more experienced.' She dared not look at Stephen as that slipped out, and she went on quickly, 'Mine was a private school and it only had three classes. I took the most junior one of the lot.'

Out of the corner of her eye she was conscious of Stephen's grin at the formality of her words; nevertheless the subject of her work was a comparatively safe one, if she managed to prevent him from getting in any of his too pointed and personal remarks.

'She won't be doing that any more, though,' Anthea chimed in gaily. 'Our Laurel will be getting married quite soon now.'

Peter showed a very flattering disappointment, but he smiled as he spoke.

'Congratulations, Miss Shannon.'

'I don't know that they're in order,' Laurel corrected, with a dry glance at Anthea. 'I rather think it's just Anthea's idea of trying her hand at matchmaking.'

'I don't think that should be too difficult.'

His eyes implied more than he put into words and Laurel felt the warm colour stain her cheeks, but she could not be offended. All she was concerned with at the moment was avoiding Stephen's glance.

'Thank you,' she managed with smiling friendliness. 'However, I don't intend to inflict myself on some unfortunate man yet awhile. I'm hoping to be able to form

54

some sort of a kindergarten school here, as Ned doesn't want me to go back to England.'

'Are you now?' Stephen murmured, and brought upon himself a glance of sharp dislike.

'Yes, I am,' Laurel retorted with some asperity. 'I've already discussed it with Mrs. Dalkeith and she thinks it an excellent idea. During school vacation I can also arrange to help them with the older children.'

Just work that out whichever way you like, Stephen Barrington! she added to herself.

The slim, dark girl who had brought the drinks before created a welcome diversion by bringing out those ordered for the men and Laurel was glad that the conversation passed from herself on to more general topics.

They talked about the climate and the rainfall – when it rained – about crops, about everything and anything, until Laurel realized that Anthea had somehow manoeuvred Peter apart and had drifted away with him, after some gaily inconsequential remark to the two left behind. Laurel, quite aware of her reasons for so doing, could have slapped her. She had no desire to have Peter removed from her vicinity so that he could not, in effect, stray into pastures that Anthea had determined should be reserved for Stephen. She had no particular interest in Peter Marshall, except for finding him a pleasant young man only a few years older than herself, but she firmly objected to the Barrington attitude of taking it for granted that they were quite at liberty to manoeuvre whoever they chose in whatever manner suited them.

'So Anthea is determined to marry you off,' Stephen commented thoughtfully.

Laurel had expected something of the sort, so she was able to shrug with comparative indifference.

'So she informed me.'

That was noncommittal enough, betraying nothing of her own feelings and, she hoped, giving Stephen nothing he could seize on.

'Has she anyone in particular in mind?'

55

She gave him a suspicious glance, but his grin did not suggest that he knew what Anthea was up to.

'Not that she mentioned,' she said carefully. Heaven forbid that he found out just who Miss Barrington did have in mind!

'That surprises me,' Stephen murmured. 'When Anthea gets ideas she usually has the full plan of campaign up her sleeve.' He slanted a rather speculative grin at her, so that for one moment she thought he actually had guessed the horrible truth. 'Sure she didn't mention anybody?'

Laurel gave him a glance that was positively arctic and hoped that it covered the sudden thudding of her heart. She felt that she would want to sink right through the beautiful mosaic of the terrace if he had the least idea of who the man was Anthea apparently intended for her – a man who, incidentally, was the last she would have chosen herself.

'Quite sure,' she said firmly, hoping that would keep him quiet. 'In any case,' she added, 'I don't like having my mind made up for me on a matter like that.'

Stephen nodded. 'You would probably refuse out of sheer perversity,' he agreed, but in such a way that she once again had the desire to hit him. Her fingers actually itched, but she knew quite well that it was something she would not give way to. Not only would it make her look like an angry fishwife, but it would probably bring quite unwelcome retribution on her unsophisticated but by no means completely ignorant head.

She shrugged and gently stroked the kitten's glossy fur. 'Anyway, Anthea will probably forget all about the idea before long,' she said with apparent carelessness.

'Probably.' Stephen straightened up off the wall with a negligent shrug, but she was quite aware that he was still watching her, losing no bit of her not too well hidden antagonism. 'You're a prickly little thing, aren't you?' he commented tolerantly after a moment, as he had once before.

'I wasn't aware of it,' Laurel retorted coldly.

'Perhaps it's just with me that you have your hackles up, then.' He surveyed her with that careless mockery she found so exasperating, one white-shod toe idly tracing a mosaic pattern. 'I wonder if you would truthfully answer me a question,' he added after a moment.

'I don't know. I suppose it depends on the question,' she said guardedly.

'Very correct and careful,' he jibed. 'You'll go far.'

'Thank you,' Laurel retorted, with what she hoped was biting sarcasm. 'Suppose you ask the question.'

His glance at her was swift, sharp and just a little unkind as well as speculative. Since the kitten chose that moment to jump off her lap and go off on pursuits of its own, she had no chance of evading that exceedingly unwelcome glance.

'I was wondering just why it is you've taken such an intense dislike to me.'

She gave him a look that clearly expressed her astonishment. 'Do you really expect me to answer that truthfully?'

'I do.'

A slow smile spread over her face. Since he had deliberately invited it and told her to answer him truthfully, it was a chance she could not stop herself accepting, to express some of her accumulated dislike, especially when there was such a lot of it mounting up – and he had only himself to blame if his vanity was injured.

'I think you're rude, overbearing and quite insufferably cynical about everything,' she stated clearly and deliberately, with every appearance of enjoying what she said. 'Also, you take a delight in twisting whatever anybody says and jeering at them.'

The words gave her a vast amount of satisfaction and a release of some of the pent-up dislike, but she nevertheless felt a little afraid when he leaned forward to stub out his cigarette. He made no move to touch her, though, merely leaned back against the same pillar that had supported him a short while ago.

'Hasn't it ever occurred to you, my child, that the cynic may envy those who still wear their rose-coloured spectacles?' he asked quietly.

She felt an odd little tremor go through her. Whatever reply she might have expected, it had not been anything like this, and she felt strangely unsure of herself now. The knowledge suddenly came to her with complete certainty that at some time in the past Stephen Barrington had been very badly hurt.

Involuntarily, her hand went out to him. 'Stephen . . .?'

'Yes, my child?' he drawled.

By imperceptible degrees the old mockery had come back over his face and she let her hand fall to her side, regretting the unthinking impulse that had sent it out to him in a swift sympathy she was now quite sure he would not appreciate.

'Nothing,' she said rather crossly. 'Nothing at all.'

It was useless trying to sympathize with him. For one moment she had actually felt an odd little pain on his behalf – which he had speedily dissipated in time to stop her saying or doing anything really foolish.

'You disappoint me. I was expecting some pearl of wisdom to fall from your lips.'

His voice was only mildly teasing this time, probably because he guessed he had successfully diverted her from a train of thought he had no intention she should follow.

'Hardly that,' she retorted. 'I'm inclined to believe now that what I was thinking was a stone of stupidity, rather than a pearl of wisdom.'

'Never that, my child.'

'And stop calling me a child!' she snapped, as a sudden rush of irritation managed to get the better of her.

Stephen grinned infuriatingly. 'That, of course, could be taken two ways.' He eyed her speculatively, his dark head a little on one side. 'One of course does not apply, as you're not a middle-aged neurotic . . .'

'Thank you,' Laurel murmured with acid sweetness.

'. . . but the other might imply that, even though a

child, you don't wish me to treat you as such,' he finished, calmly ignoring her interruption.

Just for a moment, she felt a sharp retort quivering on her lips, but she bit it back in time. Innocent of double meaning as it might appear to her, there was no way of knowing just how he might be able to twist it to get a further laugh at her expense.

'Frankly, Stephen, I couldn't care less which way you take it,' she said with a cool indifference she hoped was well assumed.

'Really?'

How on earth did he manage to put such a wealth of inflection into a single word, yet at the same time make it completely enigmatic, so that she did not have the least idea what he might be thinking, except that he was still, behind the amused grin, laughing at her youth and inexperience?

'Yes, really,' she said with a faint snap in her voice, 'and don't you think we might change the subject? I'm beginning to find it rather boring.'

'Conversation getting out of hand?'

He was jibing at her again, but this time she refused to allow herself to be goaded into retorting. She was already beginning to discover that the best way to deal with him was to let his jibes and laughing derision pass unanswered, or with a show of indifference, but it was too hard sometimes to keep a rein on her tongue in answer to the dictates of caution rather than a perfectly justified indignation.

Heaven help the girl who was unwise enough to fall in love with him! He would be able to rip her heart to shreds, yet she would always come back to be hurt again, drawn helplessly by a sharp, virile personality allied to a subtle, physical magnetism that was all the more dangerous because it was not of the more obvious kind.

For no reason at all, she shivered suddenly in the warm sunlight.

CHAPTER THREE

NED, on the way down the stairs in his small, neat house, came to a dead halt at the sound of music coming from the lounge. More slowly, he continued his interrupted journey, with a curious expression on his tanned face.

It was strange music, with an odd ethereal quality about it he could not place. Some flutelike instrument was playing a slow, plaintive melody, interspersed with the deep, booming note of a gong at regular intervals. As he opened the door and peered cautiously round the edge, Laurel was standing poised on one foot and, as her astonished and somewhat intrigued brother watched, she raised the other foot slowly, stretching and pointing it with classical grace, at the same time as she, in some incredible manner, bent over backwards with a fluidity that seemed to suggest that she was completely boneless. In that somewhat unconventional position she caught sight of her spellbound audience and flipped herself upright with swift, assured ease.

Ned came out of his trance and clapped boisterously, calling for an encore, but Laurel shook her head and went over to switch off the record. She was wearing a black leotard that left her long, slender legs and finely shaped arms bare, and Ned, more himself after the first shock of finding what he took to be a nymph dancing in his sitting-room, whistled admiringly.

'So that's what you were getting up to in England!'

Laurel smiled at his expression, which still showed some lingering surprise.

'I was just keeping in practice.' She sat down in one of the deep, comfortable armchairs, seemingly quite unaffected by the subtle exertion the slow, exquisite movements must have demanded.

'Mrs. Dalkeith was talking about arranging something

for the older children during the school vacation. I thought classical dancing might interest them,' she explained as he sat down in a chair opposite her and stretched out his long legs towards the empty fireplace.

Ned slanted her a sideways, satisfied glance. 'Made your mind up about staying, then?'

Laurel hesitated for a moment, not quite knowing how to put what she had in mind, but he settled the matter for her.

'I'm quite able to support you and give you an allowance,' he said calmly, 'and to be frank, I would prefer it that way – but knowing what a prickly and independent little squib you can be, I don't mind if you want to earn yourself some pocket money, if that's the only way to keep you here – unless of course you would prefer to live in England.'

'Don't be such an idiot. You know I would rather stay here with you.' She bit her lips and gave him an uneasy glance. 'Ned, am I really prickly?'

Ned grinned and shook his head 'Not really. You just like to stand firmly on your own two feet, I suppose.' He leaned forward with his hands clasped loosely between his knees. 'There's nobody in England for you to go back to, is there?'

Laurel blushed faintly. 'No, there's nobody there.'

'Then, if you like Ladrana, there's no reason why you shouldn't stay, unless the life here becomes too monotonous for you.' He saw her surprised, inquiring glance and added, 'It's not like living in a city, although there's still plenty of social life.'

'Ned!' she shook her head in laughing protest. 'Do you actually think my life consisted of painting the town red?' When she thought of the grubby, inkstained exercise books she laughed again. 'From what I've seen of life here already, it's far more gay than Dorminster and the annual tennis club dance.'

The inhabitants were also somewhat different. She remembered the last tennis club dance, not that they were the only social events in Dorminster, where her partner had been a slight, fair young man who left her on her doorstep with no more than a decorous and rather shy handshake, as if he would have liked to be more intimate, but did not dare to – not in the least like Stephen Barrington, who was too assured by far.

'Then I can't see any reason why you shouldn't stay here until you get married,' Ned interrupted her thoughts and his sister gave him an amused glance.

'You seem to take it for granted that I will get married.'

Ned grinned again. 'Inevitable, my pet. But until then. . . .' He made a grandiose gesture. 'My house is yours.'

Laurel rose to her feet quickly and crossed to his side to hug him with swift affection.

'I'd love to stay, Ned – and I'll try not to be too prickly and independent, if that's the way you want it.'

Both of them straightened up, a little embarrassed by the unaccustomed display of emotion, then Ned ran a hand through his fair thatch of hair with a return of his habitual grin.

'If it makes you feel any better you can designate yourself as my official housekeeper, with full union privileges,' he said with a chuckle. Another thought occurred to him. 'Or you could teach me Greek dancing.' He made an absurd and completely ungainly hop across the room. 'I think I would make a rather good nymph.'

Laurel shook her head in helpless laughter. 'Be careful! I might take you up on that.'

She half suspected that Ned, in his irrepressible mood of the moment, might have been contemplating another of those dreadful, ungraceful hops, but Pepita appeared in the doorway with her shy, old-fashioned curtsey.

'The Senhora Dalkeith, she is here.'

'Show her in,' Ned said easily, and then caught his sister's startled and faintly protesting expression, but by then Pepita had gone, in her quick, silent fashion. 'Anything wrong, pet?'

Laurel made a quick gesture towards her somewhat unconventional attire. 'I can't see visitors like this.'

Ned scratched his head. 'I don't see why not.' He could not see anything wrong with the leotard, and even though he was her brother, he was quite aware of the attractive picture she presented. He also knew that Marian Dalkeith was not in the least narrow-minded and was sure not to be shocked by the sight of slender, suntanned limbs. The lady herself settled the problem by coming into the room at that moment, ushered in by the attentive Pepita.

Marian Dalkeith smiled warmly at the two Shannons. Her greeting was pleasant and unaffected and then she added:

'You look beautifully cool, my dear. I wish I could wear a thing like that.'

Laurel glanced down apologetically at her practice costume. 'I was just about to go upstairs and change.'

Marian smiled again, with a faint twinkle in her eyes. 'I can assure you it doesn't shock me in the least,' she said. 'Some of those so-called bathing suits are only about a tenth of the size.'

They all settled down into chairs, Laurel thankful that she had not shocked someone she had come to like quite a lot, even if they had only met once before. She knew herself that there was nothing wrong with her costume; it was the conventional type of leotard worn at the Institute for practising, but she had not known Marian Dalkeith long enough to be able to judge what sort of old-fashioned ideas the elder woman might have clung to.

Marian, however, was looking at the slender limbs with obvious approval, admiring the subtle grace that was evident even in relaxation.

'I didn't know schoolteachers also taught ballet,' she said with her warm smile.

'Well, I didn't really teach it,' Laurel explained. 'It's not conventional ballet either. I joined a physical culture organization that specialized in classical Greek dancing.

Later on, when I knew more about it, I did teach some of the girls at school, for the annual concert.' She paused for a moment, then added a little diffidently, 'I was wondering whether any of the children here would be interested, that's why I was practising again.'

Marian nodded. 'It's very unusual. You should get quite a bit of support. Why not try to arrange some sort of concert? You would have no trouble in getting the proud parents to come along and see their little darlings perform.' She was a plump, middle-aged woman, but her smile became oddly impish. 'I know I would and I suspect the others would too. You might even be able to get some of the younger adults to join in.' She became serious and gave Laurel an inquiring glance. 'If you're really interested in doing something of the kind, the Milton Club Committee would help you, I'm sure. The only thing is, it would probably put a lot of work on you, and you're supposed to be having a holiday.'

'It wouldn't be work,' Laurel protested quickly. 'I love doing anything like that.'

'Then it looks as if you've elected yourself to a job,' Marian smiled. 'I think you'll find plenty of helpers, though.'

'Count me in,' Ned said, and added with his slow grin, 'Just so long as I don't have to stand on one leg and point the other at the lampshade!'

Since she could think of nothing quite so ludicrous as the sight of him in such a stance, Laurel assured him solemnly that he would be allowed to keep both feet firmly on the ground.

Ned heaved himself to his feet after a while, murmuring something about the sisal crop and that he expected they had things they wanted to say to each other without a man present.

Marian smiled as she watched him go out. 'You have a fine brother, Laurel.'

The girl nodded, with a soft light of affection in her eyes. 'I know that, Mrs. Dalkeith. I used to absolutely hero-worship him as a schoolgirl. I suppose I still do, though in a more adult way.'

'Any other man would have a job to measure up to him, I suppose,' Marian said shrewdly.

Laurel laughed lightly. 'Probably.'

'How are you getting along with Anthea?'

Laurel was glad it was Anthea Barrington who was being spoken of, not the other member of the Barrington family, or she wondered what sort of reply between tact and truthfulness she could have produced. As it was, she was able to reply with quite happy candour.

'We seem to get on quite well, although I will admit she can be annoying sometimes,' she added with a rueful grimace.

Marian nodded understandingly. 'Young Anthea quite often has decided ideas of her own.'

Distinctly odd ideas some of them were, Laurel thought, remembering Anthea's remarkable fixation on getting her married to Stephen.

'Sometimes I think Stephen must find her a bit of a handful,' Marian commented, 'but knowing Stephen, he probably copes without much trouble.'

'Oh, he would,' Laurel agreed dryly. 'I should think there would be very little he could *not* cope with.'

Marian's expression had a faintly amused tinge, but she did not comment, except to say:

'Anyway, Anthea will probably marry before very long, so somebody else will have the job of trying to keep her in some sort of order.'

Laurel thought of her brother's expression as he had spoken of Anthea Barrington and felt the same coldness she had before clutch at her heart on his behalf.

'I don't suppose she'll marry anyone on the island,' she said slowly. 'The Barringtons are so wealthy. . . .'

'They're not snobs, my dear,' Marian's voice was quiet. 'I don't think it would matter to Anthea whether the man she fell in love with had any money or not.'

'What about Stephen, though? Wouldn't he . . .?'

'He would not,' Marian broke in, with some degree of sharpness. She looked at the girl with a faint frown. 'You don't like Stephen, do you?' She paused and added, 'Why not?'

Laurel looked a little uncomfortable. 'I suppose it's because I hear so much about him,' she said diffidently. 'His manner doesn't help either. He . . . he's so cynical.'

'He has reason to be,' Marian said quietly. 'You probably don't know that he was once engaged.'

Laurel held her glance for a moment, then looked away. 'What happened?' she asked, and was surprised to find that her voice was little more than a whisper. She was also quite disturbed to feel a return of the odd, breathless pain she had felt once before, in the gardens of Castelanto, when the certainty had come to her that Stephen had been very badly hurt by someone.

'Nobody knows quite what did happen,' Marian said in her soft voice that could be sympathetic without being too obvious about it. 'He went away from here . . . it would be about seven years ago now. At that time he was full of gaiety and a kind of boyish recklessness. We heard that he had become engaged in London. When he came back to Ladrana he was changed, almost out of recognition. He was not a boy any longer and he was not engaged. He was very badly hurt, Laurel – although none of us here knows quite what happened,' she said again. 'Perhaps Anthea does. They're very close together, probably as fond of each other as you and Ned are. The next time Stephen is being aggravating – and I know he can be sometimes,' she admitted frankly. 'Just try to make allowances for him.'

She had been right, then. Somebody had hurt Stephen very badly in the past – but it was still hard to think of anybody actually being able to do so, because it seemed to her as if must always have been surrounded by that wall of cynical charm and jeering mockery – yet if Marian Dalkeith was to be believed, and Laurel felt instinctively that she was, beneath the mask Stephen was just as

66

vulnerable as anyone else.

Again she was conscious of that odd little pang on his behalf, but this time she was annoyed with herself. She was quite able to sympathize with him, like any other human being, for having been hurt, but his present attitude was not exactly conducive towards liking and she could not see herself ever feeling anything but antagonism towards him, in spite of the charm he could exert when he chose.

Laurel was surprised to find how quickly her idea caught on. It seemed that nobody on the island had ever thought about, let alone seen, such a thing as Greek dancing, and they seemed to be intrigued and interested from the first moment that they heard about it.

Marian Dalkeith turned up again the next day with a small birdlike woman who was apparently in charge of the women's section of Milton's fairly large but somewhat exclusive social club. Esme Bertram-Smythe was a little inclined towards a snobbish view of life, but since she was so genuinely interested in the new project, Laurel found herself more amused by the pretty, pert woman with her affected drawl rather than offended by some of the innocently condescending remarks.

On her second visit, three days later, she came without Marian Dalkeith but accompanied by her two daughters, one a small golden-haired angel of about five years old and the other a sun-tanned tomboy in her late teens, who had recently made her debut, with extreme reluctance, into Milton social circles. It was no secret on the island that Barbie was far happier in a pair of old shorts than dressed up and leading the social life her mother tried to force on her.

Esme Bertram-Smythe sailed into Ned's lounge like a small, important ship under full canvas. Laurel, who had been practising only ten minutes earlier, thanked her lucky stars that she had gone immediately to change.

'Good morning, Mrs. Bertram-Smythe,' she said

pleasantly, and smiled at the two children with her, although it was somewhat incorrect to call Barbie a child. She stood as tall as Laurel herself and was boyishly slim. Her skin was tanned as dark as any of the Portuguese fishermen and her shock of red, curly hair seemed to be quite unmanageable. She had the green eyes sometimes found with redheads, but they were a deep ocean green, with laughter lurking perpetually in their depths. From the moment that she came into the room Laurel took an instant liking to her.

The other Bertram-Smythe was a beautiful little sprite with huge blue eyes that she used shamelessly. Most appropriately, she was named Angela, which was naturally shortened to Angel – but Laurel wondered if she always lived up to her name. Her innocently beguiling smile sometimes had a touch of her elder sister's mischievous impudence.

Having introduced her daughters, Mrs. Bertram-Smythe settled the bunch of flowers that did duty as a hat more firmly on her head and prepared to take her departure.

'I thought I would bring them over to meet you, Miss Shannon,' she said, 'so that you can get to know each other. Unfortunately, I have to go to a committee meeting this morning, so I hope you will excuse me.'

'Of course, Mrs. Bertram-Smythe,' Laurel said politely – and was not really surprised to see Miss Barbara Bertram-Smythe give her an impudent wink behind her mother's back.

Matters eminently settled to her liking, Mrs. Bertram-Smythe took her departure, conscious that she had the means to get her younger offspring off her hands for considerable periods of many days and convinced, by that reason alone – even if no others turned up – that she was going to like Laurel Shannon.

The three left behind took stock of each other and all came to a satisfactory conclusion.

'By the way,' Miss Barbara Bertram-Smythe said,

without any unnecessary preamble, 'my friends call me Barbie.'

'And I'm Angel,' the small golden voice of the younger Miss Bertram-Smythe piped up. 'If Barbie calls you Laurel, I'm going to as well.'

'Are you now?' Laurel said with a smile. She dropped down on her knees by the child, while Barbie looked on with an amused grin. 'What makes you think I shall let you call me Laurel?'

'Oh well, you look so nice I know you will,' Angel said, with such deliberate and blatant flattery that Laurel threw Barbie a rueful glance.

'Shameless, isn't she?' Barbie said, quite unperturbed. 'The little wretch gets her own way every time, of course.'

'I don't doubt it,' Laurel replied dryly, then she smiled down at the child again. 'Have you come to learn some of my dances, Angel?'

Angel nodded. 'I want to be a sunbeam.'

At this stage Barbie, who had been sitting relaxed and happy in her chair, suddenly appeared to become slightly uneasy.

'Anything the matter?' Laurel asked, as if she had been on terms of easy friendship with the other girl for much longer than about twenty minutes.

'I'm not keen on learning these dances,' Barbie said frankly. She made a little grimace, half rueful, half deprecating. 'Please don't misunderstand me. I don't know what they're like, so I can't dislike them. It's just that dancing, or any other of the so-called social graces, doesn't seem to take kindly to me. I would be only too glad to help with anything behind the scenes, though,' she said quickly – and added with engaging candour, 'It would probably keep me occupied enough so that Mother couldn't drag me off to these wretched social engagements.'

'All right, Barbie,' Laurel said with a smile. 'If that's how you want it. Some of the dances can be pretty strenuous. You would have to really like them to endure the

69

hard practising they entail.'

'Anyone home?' a gay voice suddenly called out, and Anthea drifted in unannounced. She was dressed in a blue sun-dress that seemed to make the golden tan of her skin glow and her glorious blonde hair was tied back with a blue band. The ends of it lay on her bare shoulders in a fluff of pale chiffon and her hair had been tossed by the wind. She looked altogether too glamorous to be true, but her smile was impudent as she saw the easy relaxation of the others in the room. 'What's this – the all-girls-together session?'

'Anthea!' Angel screamed, and launched herself across the room like a miniature tornado, to clutch Anthea around bare, gold-tanned legs.

'Hey, take it easy, infant,' Anthea protested mildly, and bent down to detach the limpet who looked up at her with huge blue eyes. 'Oh lord, Barbie!' she groaned. 'Put blinkers on that child.'

'Heaven help the male sex when she grows up,' Barbie grinned.

Laurel belatedly remembered her duty as hostess. 'Come in and join us,' she said to Anthea, who was in any case already in the room. There seemed to be little formality on Ladrana, except perhaps that insisted upon by Mrs. Bertram-Smythe and her own socially conscious set. 'I was just going to have some tea made,' she added.

'Lovely. I could drink buckets.' Anthea settled herself comfortably on the couch beside Barbie. 'I think it's a wonderful idea to keep up the old English elevenses.'

Laurel only then remembered that Pepita had gone out to do the marketing and she rose to her feet to go along to the kitchen to prepare elevenses herself.

'I won't be long,' she said. 'Pepita has gone out.'

'Good. I'll come and help,' Anthea said instantly.

'I'll come too,' Barbie offered.

'I can manage all right. . . .'

Laurel found her protests cut short as they all, Angel included, escorted her out to the kitchen. Angel was told sternly to sit at the table and keep from getting under-foot. To everyone's surprise she obeyed, watching wide-eyed as the three of them, chattering gaily, brought out cups and saucers and the various other paraphernalia of tea making. After a few minutes, watching Anthea prowl happily about the kitchen, Laurel shook her head with a laugh.

'You know, you continually surprise me, Anthea. I never expected to find you at home in a kitchen.'

'The trouble is I don't manage to get there very often,' Anthea grumbled. 'I love cooking.'

'You do?'

Laurel looked so astounded that both Barbie and Anthea burst into gales of laughter.

'You know,' Anthea said, impishly mimicking Laurel's tone, 'I believe you think I'm made of sugar icing.'

'I like sugar icing,' Angel said solemnly from the table.

'Do you, pet?' Laurel said with a smile, and reached out for a cake covered with pink icing. 'There you are, then.'

'Thank you, Laurel,' Angel said indistinctly through a mouthful of cake.

'I knew it,' Anthea said triumphantly. 'Another one under her thumb!'

'Can you wonder at it?' Laurel looked over at the happy child, fast becoming covered in pink icing, and shook her head. 'If you like cooking, why don't you do more of it?' she asked, coming back to the original subject.

Anthea shuddered. 'We have an absolute gorgon of a cook at Castelanto — at least she's not exactly a gorgon,' she amended. 'I believe they say she's one of the best in this part of the world, but all she can say when I show up is "A young lady of your social position, Miss Anthea, should not concern herself with such household matters," ' and she mimicked perfectly a faintly reprov-ing elderly voice.

'No other way out, Anthea. You'll have to get mar-ried,' Barbie said jokingly.

'No fear,' Anthea retorted. 'I'm having too much fun at the moment to want to be tied down.' She threw Barbie a faintly provocative glance, as if she already knew the girl's views on the matter. 'While we're on the subject – why don't you take your own advice?'

'And get married?' Barbie gave a mock shudder. 'Heaven forbid!'

'Don't you like men?' Laurel asked.

'They make me sick,' Barbie replied succinctly. 'That is, most of them,' she added as an afterthought. 'Probably the reason why I don't like dancing is because so many of the silly idiots want to behave like grizzly bears – and if you go for a boat trip with any of them the sun goes to their head or the moon makes them amorous. All one and the same thing,' she finished with a shrug. 'They're just a darn nuisance.'

'Necessary only for the survival of the race,' Anthea tacked on for her with a grin.

'What's necessary?' Ned asked, appearing hot and dusty in the doorway.

'Men,' Anthea informed him.

'I'll say they are,' Ned agreed immediately. 'Mighty handy creatures to have around.'

'Kids himself, doesn't he?' Anthea jeered, with a glance at Laurel. She watched him amble over to the table and peer into the teapot. 'And don't think you're going to get any tea!'

'I'd better, or you'll all go out of here on your ear,' Ned retorted, and brought another cup and saucer out of the cupboard. 'Lord, was a man ever in such a position – beset by three females!'

'Stop squawking,' Anthea said inelegantly. 'You're really just loving every moment of it.'

Watching Ned. Laurel felt that he probably was. His face was split by a wide grin as he retorted in kind. It must make him happy just to have her near him, even knowing how out of reach she was; but Laurel thought of Anthea, quite at home in the small kitchen and admitting a liking for cooking, and wondered if his love for her was quite so hopeless after all – unless Stephen stood in the way, and somehow, now that she knew him better, she did not think that he would. He was still infuriating and she did not think she would ever be able to really like him, but there was no petty smallness in his nature that would make him object to his sister marrying a man who did not have as much money as she did, if he was sincerely in love with Anthea. All that, of course, depended on Anthea falling in love and also on Ned, if he was lucky enough to win her love, not standing on his dignity and refusing to ask her to marry him because she was rich and he was poor, by Barrington standards.

Oh dear, Laurel thought to herself. It all seemed to be quite a hopeless mix-up.

When they had finished the tea, refilled the pot and then emptied that as well, there was an aura of general contentment over the room.

Anthea turned her head lazily to look at Laurel. 'I came down originally to suggest that we go swimming.' She glanced at the others. 'What about it?'

Both Laurel and Barbie agreed instantly, but Ned gave a mock groan. 'What – one male among all you females? I'd be hopelessly henpecked!'

'That's what he tells us. He probably feels like a sheik surrounded by his adoring harem,' Anthea jibed.

'One of these days, young lady, you're going to get soundly smacked on a certain tender portion of your anatomy,' Ned threatened mildly.

'Want to try it, Ned darling?' Anthea asked sweetly.

'I wouldn't have the courage to.' He heaved himself up out of the chair. 'I'll clean up a bit and be back in a minute, since I've been bulldozed into this swimming party.'

Anthea muttered something in an indignant undertone and nibbled on the last remaining iced cake. Laurel had noticed before her predilection for such temptingly

73

fattening foods, but some quirk of metabolism kept her entrancingly slim. She finished the cake and licked her fingers absently, as if she was no older than Angel, then glanced over at Barbie.

'I think it might be an idea if we used the pool at Castelanto. We can keep an eye on Angel easier there.'

Barbie nodded and Angel piped up on her own behalf, 'I want to paddle in the fountain.'

'So you shall, pet,' Anthea agreed obligingly.

Ned came in a moment later, looking fresh and lanky in a white suit that somehow made him look like an overgrown schoolboy, and Laurel felt a quick rush of affection for him in her heart. Whatever else happened in life, it was good to feel that this bond would always be between them.

'Here he is, the fine upstanding figure of a man,' Anthea said impudently, with an outrageous Irish accent.

'What's the Irish accent for?' Barbie asked, as Ned made a strangling motion with his hands, as if he was wringing a chicken's neck. Anthea wrinkled her nose at him with the same provocative impudence, like a kitten tapping with a velvet paw.

They went outside to where Ned's car stood side by side with Anthea's rakish sapphire blue roadster, and after a little discussion and friendly argument they split up. Anthea driving herself and the rest in Ned's car.

They drove off, as usual in a cloud of dust, and bumped along the road until everyone gave a sigh of relief at reaching the smoother highway that led inland. Laurel remembered too well the occasion of her last drive along this road, sitting at Stephen's side trying to control her dislike and antagonism; trying to fathom out just what sort of man existed under the cynical mockery when he admitted his affection for his sister.

She was strangely eager to reach Castelanto and yet at the same time reluctant, because Stephen would be there. She tried to tell herself that both feelings did not arise from the same cause, that her eagerness was only brought into being by anticipation of the cool waters of the pool, but there was something in her heart that was not quite convinced by that argument and she was too frightened to investigate further, so she buried it deeply and gave her whole attention to talking to Angel, who was now going through a mischievous phase and climbing all over her sister like a happy puppy.

Barbie groaned, digging Angel's small but quite weighty feet out of her stomach.

'Sometimes I think Angel is a bit of a misnomer, brat,' she muttered, tenderly fingering the afflicted part of her anatomy, while Angel laughed up at her with sparkling eyes from which every vestige of solemnity had disappeared.

Laurel watched the child, completely astounded that someone like Mrs. Bertram-Smythe could have produced such an unexpected pair of offspring like Barbie and the irrepressible Angel, who on occasion definitely did not deserve her nickname. Somewhat intrigued, she wondered what the unknown and deceased Mr. Bertram-Smythe had been like.

Both cars turned at last into the well kept private road that led to Castelanto, through the brightly flowering gardens, to draw up in the now familiar patio.

There were no cats on the terrace this time, but Stephen leaned on the balustrade, idly smoking a cigarette and looking down at them. Laurel found that she was quite unable to stop her glance going immediately to his dark, pirate face and saw a hand raise in half-mocking salute as she emerged from the car. She could not think that there was anything at all personal in it, since the greeting could be meant to include all of them, but his eyes were certainly on her as he made it.

'I've brought everybody back for a swim,' Anthea announced, mounting the steps to the terrace in a swirl of blue linen and shimmering blonde hair.

'Good idea,' Stephen nodded lazily. 'I think I might

join you.'

'Thank heaven for that,' Ned said wholeheartedly. 'I was beginning to feel henpecked,' he added, and then shrank back as all three girls made threatening motions towards him.

It seemed to be one of those golden afternoons when nothing could go wrong. It started that way and just went on like it. They followed the terrace around to the back of Castelanto and down another flight of steps into a part of the gardens that Laurel wished she did not find so familiar. At least the path they took was a different one and did not end up against the low, creeper-covered wall that had stopped her flight the last time. This time, at its end, there was an ornate sunken pool, the sun glinting on its clear, sparkling water and drawing gleams of pale blue from the tiles that lined it. A low, ornate stone wall was built around the edge and at each end a small fountain tinkled into a marble bowl. A third fountain, triple-tiered, throwing out countless jets of water, almost cut the gigantic pool in half, except for a narrow channel on each side.

'Obvious why they called it the pool of fountains, isn't it?' Anthea commented.

Laurel nodded mutely, her eyes still on the great pool and the incredible fountain growing out of it. There were signs of modernization around the pool, but so skilfully done that they did not clash with what had been there far longer. A sunbathing platform had been constructed and a dressing-shed shaped like a small, ancient temple, to merge in with the creatures of legend that threw jets of water from the fountains. Small tables and chairs stood at one end of the sun platform and two diving boards, one high and the other for the not quite so brave, stood at the other end. In both sections of the pool, a round platform floated in the water and somebody, presumably Anthea, had left a gigantic and somewhat ridiculous rubber duck bobbing around in the vicinity of the centre fountain.

They undressed and slipped down into the caressing warmth of the water. Anthea was wearing a two-piece white costume and had bundled her blonde hair up beneath a tight-fitting cap, but Barbie, boyish and lithe in a plain black costume, went into the water with her head bare, like Laurel, who for a moment, when she encountered Stephen's faint grin, felt selfconscious in her own plain green costume. As she slipped quickly into the water she was sure that she heard him murmur something about schoolteachers.

Stephen himself looked more than ever like a pirate, his tanned skin gleaming in the sunlight and the black hair wet and sleek as a seal's.

They splashed around in the water for a while, then the men left them for the deeper half of the pool, where the diving boards were. Angel paddled in the small fountain at the end of the pool her sister occupied and was quite happily engaged there until she saw Anthea astride the absurd rubber duck, then she had to be brought into the pool to be given a ride.

Eventually they tired themselves out and lay down on the sun platform, talking in the lazy, desultory fashion of people warmed by the sun and quite content with life as it was at the moment, whatever came afterwards, until one of the servants came down to them with the news that a Senhor Manoel de Valente had arrived.

For a moment Laurel saw the imperturbable Stephen shaken off balance by surprise.

'Manoel!' He came to his feet quickly, with a nod of dismissal to the man who had brought the news, then glanced down at the others. 'No need to break up the party. Manoel will probably join us.'

He did not stop to dress, but merely belted a short towelling robe around him and went towards the house. From the informality of his attire – and Stephen knew when to be formal and when not to be – Laurel guessed that the unexpected visitor was someone close to the family. It was not until Barbie spoke that she remembered that Anthea had once mentioned somebody by the name of Manoel and realized that the name of Valente was also familiar.

'Who is this Manoel de Valente?' Barbie asked, with an inquiring glance at Anthea.

'A sort of cousin, I suppose – very far removed,' Anthea informed her. She wrinkled up her brows in a faint frown, then shrugged. 'I never have been able to work out the exact relationship. It's probably so remote as to be non-existent, but we like to consider him one of the family. His people are decended from the son of old Dom Miguel who built Castelanto,' she added, and then Laurel remembered just where and when it had been that she had heard the name Valente before.

Barbie appeared to be indulging in a little frowning thought. 'I think I remember meeting him once before,' she said slowly. 'It was at your eleventh birthday party. Wasn't he the horribly fat little boy who sat in a corner all the afternoon and looked startled when anyone came near him.'

Anthea laughed. 'That's him – but, my pet, he's changed out of all recognition, although he's still as shy as he ever was. He came to my twenty-first birthday party as well, when you were over in England. I tried to flirt with him, but. . . .' she grinned impishly, 'the poor boy almost blushed!'

Laurel shook her head with a whimsical smile. 'Now what happens to all my ideas of the bold, bad Latin?'

Anthea rolled over on to her stomach with a chuckle and dug her toes luxuriously into the foam rubber she lay on.

'I have an idea Cousin Manoel might be a little hard to handle if he was really roused. He seems so shy and easy-going I sometimes wonder how he's managed to avoid the hooks,' she added pensively. 'There have been plenty of matchmaking mammas and designing daughters after him, but somehow he has drifted clear.'

There was the sound of footsteps coming along the

path that led to the house, and then Stephen came in sight with another man walking by his side. If Manoel de Valente had been fat as a boy there was no sign of it now. He was of medium height and slimly built, carrying himself with quiet, unobtrusive pride, the type of man, Laurel thought, one likes on sight. His features were almost thin, sensitively carved, with a Latin darkness that was not too heavily swarthy. The same sensitivity was in the curve of his mouth – and she could not help comparing it with the ruthlessness of Stephen's and the hint of cruelty she had noticed before and hoped she never came up against again.

Manoel acknowledged the introductions with a faint bow and a murmur of something instinctively courteous and fitting for the occasion, reserved without being remote and very attractive in his slightly shy composure. Anthea's words seemed to indicate that he was very eligible for more than his looks, and Laurel did not have to look far to find the answer as to how he had avoided the snares set for him. The shyness of his dark eyes was not altogether unworldly and there was a determined firmness to his clean-shaven chin. Manoel de Valente probably had quite a will of his own, unobtrusive though it might be.

Anthea he greeted as cousin, in spite of the fact that the relationship was far removed, and Laurel found herself the recipient of a pleasant, friendly smile; but when he turned to Barbie there was a faint ripple, almost of shock, over his features. His eyes narrowed and there was a flicker of some inexplicable light in their darkness, before he was again the polite, charming guest.

Barbie did not seem to have noticed, nor did any of the others, and for a moment Laurel wondered if her imagination was playing tricks on her – or for one brief second she really had witnessed something she had not quite believed in – the proverbial love at first sight.

'What brings you to Ladrana?' Stephen inquired with casual friendship.

Manoel shrugged, with a negligent gesture of one slim hand. 'No reason, my friend – except perhaps to make a nuisance of myself,' he added with a surprisingly boyish grin.

'Never that,' Anthea murmured softly, slanting a look up at him through curling lashes, half teasing, half provocative in her irrepressible delight in flirting with almost any attractive and unattached man she liked the look of.

By her side Laurel felt Ned stiffen and forced herself not to look round at him. She knew he had been hurt by the softly murmured words and the blue glance Anthea had given the young Portuguese, but she knew too that she could never dislike the younger girl. She could understand only too well why Ned loved her. Anthea Barrington was like a gaily coloured butterfly, flitting lightheartedly in the sunlight, but one day she would come to rest and whoever held her then would hold the flame of life itself.

At that moment Angel, who had fallen asleep some time ago, temporarily quietened and exhausted by her paddling and more strenuous efforts in the pool, even though supported by adults, came drowsily awake and to the awareness that there was a stranger present. For a moment she fixed him with huge, wondering eyes and then bestowed on him a melting smile that brought a groan of protest from Anthea.

'Cut it out, infant. Not him too!' Her glance at Angel's sister was almost pleading. 'Blinkers, Barbie, I insist!'

Barbie gave her unaffected tomboy grin. 'Might be an idea.'

Angel, however, decided to go back to sleep and promptly lay down again on her own foam rubber cushion. Within seconds her bewitching eyes had closed and she had lost interest in everyone around her.

Manoel laughed, 'It seems that she finds us of little interest.' His smiling glance went to Barbie. 'She is an enchanting child, Miss Bertram-Smythe.'

'Lord, what a mouthful!' Anthea cut in inelegantly. 'You'd better call her Barbie. Everyone else does.'

'With your permission, Barbie?'

'Of course.' Barbie nodded towards the sleeping child. 'The brat is called Angel with those eyes, but she doesn't always live up to her name.' Her glance at Angel, though, was affectionate and it was quite evident to everyone that, however much Angel might not live up to her name, her elder sister would never allow anyone else to comment on her often unangelic behaviour.

The conversation became general, sliding easily from one topic to another. Manoel, it seemed, had been to the mainland on his yacht, which was moored in Milton's harbour at the moment, and had decided to pay a call on his relatives on the way back.

After a time Anthea yawned and stretched. 'I feel hungry,' she said, and jumped to her feet with surprising energy considering the languor of her yawn. 'Suppose we all go inside now for lunch.'

Barbie uncurled herself and directed a glance at the sleeping Angel.

'Don't worry about her. I'll keep an eye on her while you dress,' Stephen offered, and fell into conversation with Manoel. Laurel was surprised to hear him speaking fluently in a language she guessed to be Portuguese. It had a pleasant, musical sound and she glanced at him with quick curiosity. For once he did not notice, and she was able to turn and accompany Anthea and Barbie into the dressing pavilion without any unwelcome comment in his mocking, too-perceptive manner.

They showered and dressed and then set about the more serious business of making themselves presentable to the male audience outside. Barbie merely flicked a comb through her damp curls and outlined her young mouth lightly with lipstick, the latter action carried out as if it was against her will and only bowed down to through parental insistence. Murmuring something about seeing how Angel was getting on, she wandered out, leaving Anthea more carefully combing out her own long fair hair.

Laurel herself was also ready, her skin softly tanned and glowing, her tobacco brown hair a shining mass of damp curls, but Anthea started chattering to her immediately Barbie went out, so she remained in the room, watching the younger girl uncap a brilliant pink lipstick.

As on that other memorable occasion, the first time she had visited Castelanto, she watched Anthea swivel round in her chair before the mirror, the lipstick, still unused, held between her slender fingers.

'Know something?' she said suddenly. 'I think Manoel has fallen for our Barbie.'

So it had not been imagination. Anthea at least had noticed, and if she had it was probable that Stephen had also come to the same conclusion, since there was very little that he missed.

'What do you think?' Anthea asked, watching her speculatively and making it clear that she expected an answer.

'I don't know,' Laurel began hesitantly. 'I didn't really believe it could happen quite like that.'

'Oh, it can,' Anthea assured her. 'Pouf! Just like that!' She snapped her fingers to illustrate.

Laurel gave her a faintly whimsical smile. 'Lot you would know about it,' she retorted.

'Oh, I've heard of it happening before,' Anthea said airily. She gnawed on her lips with pensive satisfaction. 'It's really quite the best thing that could have happened.'

'What is?'

Anthea threw her a surprised glance, as if the other girl should have known quite well what was in her mind. In any event, Laurel did have some intuition of what was coming.

'Why, Manoel falling in love with Barbie, of course. She'll make him a wonderful wife.'

'And what's Barbie going to say about it?' Laurel inquired dryly. 'You know how she regards men.'

'Oh, she'll get over that.' Anthea dismissed that aspect of the matter quite blithely. 'I wonder how long Manoel will stay here, though. We may have to work quickly.'

Laurel's eyes widened in dismay. 'Oh no!' she said quickly. 'Not again, Anthea!'

Anthea gave her a gaily defiant glance. 'Why not?'

'No girl likes matchmaking going on behind her back. It's humiliating to be thrown at a man's head.'

'Heavens above, I don't do it with brickbats!' Anthea said indignantly. 'I think I've managed things very well so far.' A provocative and teasing smile turned her lips. 'In fact, I'm quite satisfied with progress. Aren't you?'

Laurel bit back a sharp retort. 'I wasn't aware that any progress had been made,' she evaded.

'Don't tell me you still dislike him.'

Laurel remained silent, but her expression was answer enough, as it had been once before, and Anthea shook her head wonderingly.

'I just don't get it. He's good-looking and I'd stake my life on it that he makes love in an extremely acceptable way.'

'Anthea! Don't be so . . .' Laurel began indignantly, but Anthea cut across her words.

'And don't you be such a prude,' Anthea retorted.

'What makes you think it's acceptable, then?' Laurel demanded, with a faint snap in her voice.

'How would you know?' Anthea was teasing again, but her eyes widened in sudden delighted surprise at the flush Laurel could not control. 'Don't tell me!' she breathed softly.

Laurel came to her feet swiftly, with taut, restrained anger. 'I have no intention whatsoever of telling you anything,' she said coldly, and started to walk towards the door. 'I suggest that it's about time we joined the others.'

Anthea came up out of her chair, her hands outstretched in a sweet, unaffected gesture. With a few quick steps she caught hold of Laurel's hands.

'Please, Laurel! I'm sorry. I know I sometimes speak out of turn. . . .'

'Why do you do it, then? Why do you try and arrange other people's lives?'

Laurel felt her anger evaporating and was quite powerless to stop it, even though she felt also that she should take a firm stand.

Anthea made a little deprecating movement. 'I suppose it's because when I like someone I want them to find happiness with someone nice.' She dropped her eyes, which had become more serious than Laurel had ever seen them before, and her voice was little more than a whisper. 'I adore Stephen. I . . . I think I would do anything for him. He was hurt very badly once. I don't want it to happen again.'

Laurel made no mention of the fact that Marian Dalkeith had already given her an intimation of some such episode in the past.

'You can't stop him being hurt by trying to arrange his life,' she pointed out quietly. 'In any case, Stephen is quite able to look after himself. I'm sure he wouldn't like any interference, especially when it's such a personal matter.'

'I suppose not,' Anthea agreed, although reluctantly. She turned back to the mirror and at last began to apply lipstick with a careful hand. Laurel stood by the doorway, watching her and thinking about the woman who had somehow managed to hurt Stephen Barrington. It seemed incredible to her, knowing him as he was now, that such a thing had ever been possible, but she was sure from her own knowledge now that it had happened. There had been that moment, quickly restrained, when she had put out her hand to him in sympathy, with an odd desire to ease the hurt that he hid so well behind the mask of worldly cynicism and the mocking sharpness of his eyes. She had been certain then.

Now it was strangely doubled, that silly urge to help a man who she was sure would scorn any such offer, the desire to ease pain that she was at the same time just as sure he had himself banished and if it ever recurred regarded it with detached mockery until it was sent on its way again.

Anthea's voice interrupted her thoughts, as the younger girl turned round from the mirror again. There was a faintly whimsical half-deprecating smile on her face.

'What about Barbie? Am I allowed to get my sticky fingers in there?'

'Must you?' Laurel asked reasonably. 'Why not let things just run their course?'

To her relief Anthea seemed to agree with her, although she said nothing. At least her expression was not complete disagreement.

'Just so long as that Bertram-Smythe woman doesn't try to marry her off to any money-bagged ancient,' she said after a moment, in rather a tart voice. Her glance slid to Laurel with a hint of Stephen's mockery. 'Don't look so shocked. You've seen enough of Mrs. B-S to know what she's like. Her main idea is to get Barbie married off to money, irrespective of the man tacked on to the cheque book. Can you wonder I want to interfere?' she finished explosively, and jumped to her feet. 'I think you're right. We'd better join the others or we might come to blows.'

Laurel smiled and shook her head. 'Pax! We won't fight over it. Personally I think Barbie is far too sensible a girl to let her mother push her into any marriage that's distasteful to her. At the moment it's quite obvious that she has no interest in the subject, but if Manoel really should fall in love with her he might be able to make her change her mind. Let's leave it at that, shall we?'

During lunch, in the course of conversation, Manoel informed them that his yacht would be anchored off Ladrana for some time, and Anthea, with all her usual gaiety, insisted that they should have a small party, just the six of them, that evening, to celebrate his arrival. Barbie was the only one who hesitated to acclaim it a good idea, but her pleasing recollections of the day she had spent at Castelanto very quickly won her over.

Angel, wide awake and beginning to give the lie to her name, was hoisted unceremoniously on to her sister's shoulder and carried out to Ned's car.

During the drive, the deviation that they had to make to reach the Bertram-Smythe house took them to the top of a hill. Below them, in the distance, Milton lay spread out, with the arms of its harbour encircling the few ships in port. There was a newcomer there now, a slender white yacht they guessed belonged to Manoel.

'That must be Manoel's yacht,' Barbie said, putting the thought into words. She leaned forward, peering downwards. 'This must be visitors' day. There's another yacht just outside the harbour. I wonder if it will be stopping here, or just sailing by.'

Laurel followed her glance and saw it, a craft that looked small and insignificant with distance – but for some reason she had an unaccountable pang of apprehension. Then it was gone, as quickly and as suddenly as it had appeared, and she shrugged, dismissing it from her thoughts and turning aside to give the whole of her attention to Anthea and the arrangements that were being made for the evening.

It was an evening Laurel remembered for a very long time. Lately she had been leading a fairly social life, and by contrast with her life in England it was certainly eventful. She found herself meeting people – some of them pleasing, some of them not so pleasing. Mrs. Bertram-Smythe was amongst the 'not so pleasing', and Stephen Barrington had the distinction of being the only one on the island of Ladrana who had aroused her wholehearted hostility.

But even the hostility she felt for Stephen had faded a little with the passing of the days. She could feel sorry for him now, since she knew that he was in a sense vulnerable, and in order to feel sorry for a person you had to cease feeling violently antagonistic towards them.

After they returned to Ned's cottage she was still not quite sure – in fact, very far from sure – why the evening that loomed ahead of her was not entirely distasteful. In fact, if she was truthful, she was looking forward to it. . . . And she spent a lot of time selecting a dess to wear that would do justice to it and give her confidence which was far more important, really, than that she should create a good impression.

She and Ned had a swift drink when they got back, and then there was a scramble for the bath-hut. Naturally, in the end, Ned gave way graciously to his sister, and while he was still coping with his toilet she sat waiting for him in the sitting-room, touching up her nails with an attractive dusky peach-coloured varnish, and looking infinitely alluring and at the same time deliciously simple in white broderie anglaise.

As usual Ned pretended to be quite literally bowled over at sight of her, and then he walked across the room and dropped a kiss lightly on her tobacco brown curls.

'You look adorable, infant,' he told her. 'If that fellow Manoel doesn't eat out of your hand tonight I shall be amazed.'

She smiled at him, dimpling as she did so.

'I'm not interested in that fellow Manoel.'

'No?' He slanted a curious glance at her. 'Then who—?'

'No one.' She continued to dimple and to look demure. 'I dress to please myself, and if I look nice . . . well, that pleases me! I don't bother about anybody else.'

He looked, she thought, a little dubious, but as they were rather late he didn't pause to argue the matter, but insisted that they went out to the car. It was perfectly clear to Laurel that he was counting the moments until he could feast his eyes on Anthea again.

Laurel felt a little odd as they neared the Portuguese-type house of the Barringtons. Earlier in the day, when she saw the yacht in the harbour, she had experienced the same sort of oddness. But now it seemed to be reinforced. She had never encouraged the idea that she possessed a kind of sixth sense, but the Shannons as a family were known to be fey. For one moment as they arrived in the patio of Castelanto she wanted to urge Ned almost frantically to start the car up and take them home again. But she managed to get the better of the impulse.

Even Ned seemed to think that the home of the Barringtons was blazing with rather more light than usual. The whole of the west front, where the main bedrooms were situated, was a sequence of lighted windows, and drawn up in the patio there were two long and powerful cars.

'I don't think I've seen either of those before,' Ned remarked, as he helped his sister alight.

'I expect one of them belongs to Manoel,' Laurel replied, and Ned accepted it as rather more than likely.

'Normally I wouldn't wonder,' he said, 'only Anthea said there were to be only the six of us.'

It was quite plain, the moment they entered the house, that its atmosphere had undergone a change. There was a feeling of excitement ... of tension as well. So many voices seemed to be talking at once that Ned glanced at Laurel and lifted his eyebrows.

Anthea came running down the staircase to greet them. She looked brilliantly beautiful in a flaunting scarlet dress, and Laurel noticed in a vague sort of way that there were diamonds at her neck and wrists. Her expression was both gay and arch, and at the same time it seemed to Laurel that her eyes were fixed on her so intently that she actually thought they were appealing to her.

'Darlings,' and she gestured with her hands, 'we've got a surprise for you. This really is a day of days! First Manoel turns up unexpectedly this morning, and now the whole house is full! You remember the other yacht we saw this morning? Well, her owner and his guests are old friends, and they're staying with us! Isn't it marvellous?'

There was undoubtedly something feverish about her expression, and her flow of speech was like a bubbling mountain stream. She gestured to the group behind her, and out of them all Laurel picked one woman – a graceful, exquisite creature with red-bronze hair and cool eyes, who appeared to be watching her with interest despite the fact that Stephen was engaging her in conversation – and concentrated all her attention upon her, as if she knew without having it explained to her that here was someone fate had intended her to meet, and as a result of their meeting nothing was ever going to be quite the same again.

She saw Anthea turn to her and call her by name: 'Come here, Roberta, you've *got* to meet Laurel and Ned – and particularly Laurel!'

The others were admiring the hall and its graceful proportions, and it was Ned who counted heads swiftly and realized there were five of them. Three beautifully turned-out men— one of them very tall and fair, like a Viking – and two charmingly dressed women, who seemed genuinely attracted by the Portuguese architecture and impressed by the array of portraits in the gallery.

The woman called Roberta, who was splendidly tanned and wearing white slipper satin that contrasted arrestingly with her tan, said something laughingly to Stephen and moved across the hall to stand at the side of her youthful hostess, and it was then that Anthea made the announcement that must have shaken Stephen, and very nearly floored Laurel.

'They were going to keep it secret until dinner tonight ... but I simply can't wait! Roberta, you've got to be the first to offer your congratulations. This is Stephen's fiancée, Laurel Shannon!'

CHAPTER FOUR

For one awful moment Laurel thought she was suffering the ill effects of too much powerful and unaccustomed sun that day. And then, while Ned's eyes fixed themselves upon her as if he, too, suspected they had been overdoing things that day, she heard Anthea rushing on with her introductions.

'Laurel, this is Mrs. Franson, a very old friend of Stephen's.' There was no doubt about it, she underlined the words 'a very old friend of Stephen's' with deliberate emphasis, and her eyes didn't merely appeal to Laurel, they actually sought to compel her in some wild way. She probably knew she was burning her own boats and almost certainly risking quite a violent scene if Laurel chose to be unco-operative and insisted on denying such an outrageous statement. But before Laurel could even formulate the words that would have revealed the truth to Roberta Stephen stepped forward and made it impossible for her to do so.

'Annoying brat!' he accused his sister. 'You even have to deny me the thrill of announcing my own engagement!'

He swung round and reached for Laurel's hand, drew it through his arm, and then bowed to the entire assembly of his guests. 'All right, then, you can go ahead with your congratulations! We'll celebrate before dinner!'

They all crowded round, the latest contingent of visitors Manoel, Barbie, Ned. Barbie accused Stephen of being a dark horse, and Ned quite plainly could not have been more delighted once his astonishment passed.

'Well, I'm damned!' he declared, and would have separated his sister from Stephen in order to hug her and give her his blessing, but for the fact that Stephen refused to allow Laurel to be detached from his side. He kept tight hold of her hand that was resting nervously in the crook of his arm, and when she looked as if she needed a little support he freed her hand and put his arm about her. She would never have believed that the feel of Stephen's arm supporting her would give her courage. ... But when she needed it most, and in her bewilderment, affected as she was by a sense of outrage, and horrified at the same time because she was a pretty poor actress, and she knew it, the steel-strong pressure of his arm in a white dinner-jacket sleeve filled her with the sort of gratitude she would have felt if someone had flung her a lifeline when she was drowning.

'Smile,' he commanded, with audacious calmness, for her ear alone, and she smiled. She glanced up desperately into his face, and his grey eyes were looking down at her with a star-like glitter peeping at her between his eyelashes, while at the same time the lines of his mouth were firm – but gentle. With nothing else to preoccupy her she could have been amazed by that gentleness, because it even occurred to her that there was a kind of protective tenderness at the corners of his mouth as well.

But that could have been entirely due to her imagination.

They went through into the drawing-room, where champagne cocktails were handed out to the guests, and Laurel found herself sipping hers with a shaking hand clutching the stem of the glass. Roberta Fransom came and stood near her, and although she said nothing at all she smiled in a most peculiar way. It was a smile that made Laurel feel she couldn't possibly carry on with this piece of deception when she encountered it.

'When did it all happen?' Ned wanted to know in his innocent way.

'The first day Laurel arrived,' Stephen replied, so promptly that Laurel stared at him with her mouth very nearly dropping open.

'The first day?' That was Barbie, expressing quite understandable surprise. 'That makes it love at first sight,' she commented, with extraordinary complacency considering her present attitude to romance.

'Yes, it does, doesn't it?' Anthea pretended to look incredulous. 'But these things do happen, of course!'

'Only very, very rarely, in my experience,' Mrs. Fransom observed from the middle of a priceless Persian rug near the fireplace.

She and Stephen exchanged glances that no one else in the room – except Laurel – observed.

Laurel listened with a feeling of complete unreality to the fascinating story of how she and Stephen had fallen in love, and she was so bemused by the turn events had taken that she almost believed it herself as she listened. Stephen undoubtedly enjoyed himself for some reason as he held forth on the subject, and the fact that his sister's eyes were anxious whenever they rested upon him did nothing to effect the charm of the story for the assembled guests, ... but it explained a good deal to Laurel. Anthea was half afraid of her brother, but she was also devoted to him and knew him very well, and it quite plainly struck her that he was either over-acting, or she didn't know him quite as well as she thought.

Whenever she met Laurel's eyes Anthea's were still pleading ... and for no sensible reason that she could think of – not even any practical reason – Laurel refrained from letting her down.

The whole of dinner was taken up with talk of the engagement, and after dinner, while the ladies waited for the gentlemen to join them, Laurel had to submit to a good deal of quizzing on the part of Barbie. Anthea was not unnaturally more considerate, and Mrs. Fransom was plainly not very much addicted to light conversation. She preferred to curl up gracefully in the corner of a settee and smoke one of her own cigarettes in a long and obviously expensive holder, and study Laurel thoughtfully from a distance. The thoughtfulness of her look was so marked that Laurel was even glad when the men came in and, as if by right, Stephen attached himself to her side.

He bent and pulled her upwards out of her chair.

'I want Laurel to myself in order to show her her engagement ring,' he said, displaying a remarkable aptitude for invention, and his fingers closed tightly around her arm as he led her to the door. 'Come along, darling,' he murmured suavely, to defeat at source any desire she might have to rebel. 'I'm sure the others will excuse us under the circumstances.'

Laurel, however, had no desire at all to resist accompanying him. This thing had gone on long enough, she thought, and the sooner they were alone together to have it out the better. So meekly she allowed him to lead her out of the room and along a corridor to a room she had not so far visited. It was Stephen's own private sanctum, and only when they were safely inside it and he had taken the precaution of locking the door on the inside did he release her hand.

Laurel rubbed the mark on her wrist that his hard fingers had caused, and looked about his room with a flickering of interest. It was handsome and book-lined, and much as she would have expected Stephen's private retreat to be like, but apart from that it had no interest for her. Certainly not at the moment.

Stephen thrust her down into one of the deep leather armchairs, offered her a cigarette which she declined, and astounded her by asking grimly:

'Now, would you mind telling me what all this is about?'

'Would I mind telling you . . .?' she began indignantly. 'I was just about to ask you that question!'

He made a slight movement of his hand. 'All right, don't fly off the handle. I just wondered. I might have known it was completely Anthea's handiwork.'

Laurel nodded, feeling some relief that at least she was exonerated from any complicity. It helped matters to know that he did not blame her. For once his mocking amusement had completely disappeared, and it was not to be wondered at. His dark, pirate face was serious and even slightly grim.

'Why on earth didn't you deny it?' she asked without

thinking.

'And make the lot of us look like a pack of idiots?'

'I suppose so,' she admitted reluctantly. 'I can't think what made Anthea say such a crazy thing.'

'Can't you?' Stephen said with a shade of grimness. 'I think I can. The problem is, what are we going to do about it?'

Laurel felt that she had nothing whatsoever to contribute, so she remained silent, in case she merely said something stupid, because she could see no way out of the tangle save that of admitting to everyone that the engagement had been in Anthea's mind alone.

'Well?'

'Couldn't we pass it off as a joke?' she suggested tentatively.

'Too late now.' He shook his head decisively. 'I doubt whether it would have smoothed things over even at the time.' He became silent for a moment, then straightened up off the desk. 'Only one thing for it – we'll have to go on with it.'

'*What*?'

A shade of his old mocking grin returned as he looked down at her completely incredulous expression.

'Don't start getting scared. I meant we only have to keep it up for a short time. I don't imagine you really want to marry me.'

'About as much as you want to marry me,' Laurel retorted. She saw one dark brow jerk up in the too familiar fashion and added hastily, 'How long would it have to go on for?'

'Just long enough for you to get tired of me and seek fresh pastures.'

'And how long does it take for a girl like me to grow tired of a man like you?' she asked, with her tobacco-brown head a little on one side as she looked up at him.

He answered coolly.

'I can't answer that, because I've never known a girl like you before.'

94

'Oh!' She gave him a curious glance. 'You're not afraid I might try and hang on to you instead of letting you go. Sue you for breach of promise?'

His face looked suddenly almost deadly.

'Try it,' he said.

She looked away from him. He actually made her shiver inwardly.

'Well, it's a situation that could be fraught with danger for you,' she insisted on pointing out. 'The rich and eligible Stephen Barrington supposedly engaged to a school-teacher.'

He smiled very faintly.

'I'm not afraid,' he admitted.

'Well,' she sat back in her chair, 'what do we do now? Go back to the others?'

'I suppose so.' Unexpectedly he bent and lifted her chin with his thumb and finger. 'Think you can pretend to be in love with me?'

By the warmth of her cheeks she knew that she blushed. 'I can only try,' she countered.

'And you'd better make a good job of it,' he warned, his expression strangely serious. 'If I think you're not trying hard enough I shall kiss you in front of everybody. Understood?'

'Understood,' she echoed, obviously recoiling before the threat.

Before they left the room he remembered the reason why they were alone.

'I almost forgot,' he said. 'I brought you here to show you your ring!'

He produced a small key from his pocket, and went across to a picture that hung on the wall and pushed it aside to reveal a safe. Laurel watched fascinatedly as he unlocked the safe, thrust in his hand, and then turned round to her again with a small jewel case in his hand. He snapped back the lid to reveal a large, square emerald set between two small diamonds, sending out shafts of green fire from a bed of velvet. He reached for her hand, but she drew back.

'Stephen! Am I supposed to wear that?'

'Well, I don't exactly intend to wear it myself.' He gave her an inquiring glance. 'What's the matter? Don't you like it? We can have a look for something else if you'd rather.'

He was already turning back towards the safe, but impulsively she caught at his arm.

'It's beautiful, but I can't wear it,' she protested. 'I should be afraid of losing it.'

'Don't be ridiculous.'

Before she could protest any further he slid the ring on to her finger, where it sparkled expensively, quite unlike the sort of ring she had visualized herself wearing if she ever did get engaged to be married. Then, with his hand beneath her elbow, they passed out of the room and back along to the corridor to the room where all his friends, and his sister, were awaiting them.

Laurel had to submit to having her hand examined and the ring admired, and all the time she tried to look like a happily engaged young woman who had no reservations whatsoever about the man she was to marry. And somehow she managed to pull it off in a way that surprised her more than anything else had ever surprised her in life, and Stephen actually applauded her in an approving whisper at one stage.

'You're doing splendidly! Keep it up!'

The carpet was rolled back and they danced as they had danced on her first visit to Castelanto, and Laurel felt she was moving in a dream as she danced with her brand-new fiancé. She tried to get Anthea alone when they both went to renew their make-up in a corner of the powder-room in between one of the dances, but Miss Barrington was exceptionally wily tonight and succeeded in evading her when one of the other women from the yacht came in.

They all descended the wonderful sweeping staircase to the dance room, and that was the last opportunity

Laurel had that night to have a highly necessary word with Anthea.

She danced several dances with Stephen, and once again he congratulated her on the wonderful show she was putting up.

'At this rate you'll even convince me that I'm engaged to be married!'

They circled the floor, and he held her very tightly — quite plainly in order to keep up the deception. She was feeling a little light-headed, as if the champagne cocktails before dinner and the excellent Portuguese wine that had been served with dinner had gone to her head.

'Yes, it was pretty good, wasn't it?' she acknowledged, peeping at him under her lashes. 'But with such a threat hanging over my head I had to make an effort,' she added.

He laughed softly, understanding that she was referring to his threat to kiss her.

'Touché, my child,' he murmured, and held her away from him and looked down at her with a slightly quizzical expression. 'Was it such a dire threat?'

'Well, the last occasion was not exactly pleasant,' she countered, and wondered why they were on such apparently good terms now when she knew very well of what he was capable if provoked. Every time she glanced at him she was provoking him, and unless she was very careful something she said would recoil on her.

'You asked for it,' Stephen's voice broke into her thoughts. 'I suppose it would be too much to ask just what did make you behave like a prickly cactus that evening?'

'Poison ivy,' Laurel corrected, resorting to evasion. After all, the reason for her behaviour that night was Ned's secret and not hers to give away. She had half a hope that he might leave the matter there, but it quickly died when he spoke, as she would have known had she thought about it for any length of time.

'Poison ivy, then,' he conceded. 'Now, out with it. Just

what did cause the prickles?'

'Prickles – now we're back to cactus,' she evaded yet again, because she did not have the faintest idea what to say. It was, of course, quite impossible to tell him the real reason and just as impossible to think up anything else that would sound reasonable and not too insulting. She did not want to quarrel with him and it was not just because such a situation would only make it more difficult to act out the pretence they were caught up in. It was a definite knowledge in her mind, stemming from the same source that gave rise to the other odd feelings she had acknowledged only a short time ago. It hurt quite sharply, she found, to see his dark face close up, as he recognized her second evasion.

'All right, my child, I won't beat it out of you.'

Impulsively her hand tightened on his shoulder. 'Stephen. . . .'

'Yes?'

His voice was noncommittal and faintly withdrawn. She wished she could see his face, but he was looking over her shoulder with apparent disinterest in what she had to say, although she guessed he was probably still wearing an appropriate expression for the rest of the room to see.

Again on impulse, before she could think about it and decide otherwise, she moved slightly and lifted her head, so that she could look up into his face. Under those circumstances he had no choice but to bring his glance round to her and a faint, amused smile twitched his lips as he saw the seriousness of her expression.

'Is it as bad as that?'

'It's something . . . you see, it doesn't only concern me,' she said haltingly. 'I managed to get quite a wrong idea into my head and I intended to be deliberately unpleasant,' she added with a frankness that was engaging, only she did not realize it, only wondered what caused his smile to change in such a subtle way that she could not exactly define the difference. 'I can't tell you what it was, but I do really feel sorry for being such ... such a piece of poison ivy,' she concluded with a smile '... and I want to apologize.'

'I suppose, in that case, I shall also have to apologize for my retaliatory actions,' Stephen commented.

'And so you should,' his make-believe fiancée retorted. 'If I have to be kissed I don't see why I shouldn't enjoy it.'

Laurel felt quite astounded as she heard the words pass her lips, especially as she was sure he could twist it whichever way he pleased if he happened to mercurially change to one of his mocking, dangerous moods. It was like sailing a tiny ship into rather turbulent waters, knowing that the waves could swamp it, or playing with fire and daring the flame. To counter the menace, there was a peculiar, bubbling recklessness in her that had started to grow from the moment she came back into the room with Stephen's ring on her finger and met Roberta's jewel-green eyes; and if this rather dangerous sparring had the effect of causing Mrs. Fransom, who was one of his oldest friends, to think that Stephen and herself were thoroughly absorbed in each other, all the better.

'I can do much better, you know,' Stephen said, accepting the challenge of her words, just as she had known he would, and the music finished at that moment, giving her no chance to reply, since Barbie, who had been dancing with Manoel, was right at their side.

There was a short interval that taxed her ingenuity while people asked Stephen and herself their plans for the future. She was repeatedly amazed at his easy command of the extremely difficult situation, at the smooth evasions with which he turned a too pertinent inquiry aside; then there was a slight respite as she found herself dancing with Manoel. The young Portuguese was a smooth, graceful dancer and so quietly attractive that, as Anthea had done earlier, she decided he and Stephen made the other men in the room look mere background, apart from the Viking-fair man who was so magnificently tall. He had been too glibly courteous and charming when he had been introduced to her and offered congratulations on her coming marriage. Ned, of course, she put in a different class from all of them, although even she had to admit that his sun-browned, good-natured face could not compete with the pirate mockery of Stephen's aquiline features or Manoel's dark attraction.

At the thought of him, she turned her head slightly to look for Stephen and found him dancing with Roberta. A quick coldness stabbed at her heart and a premonition of danger, although she was not at all sure what form it would take.

She shivered faintly and Manoel looked down at her in quick, courteous concern.

'You are cold?'

Laurel shook her head instantly, wondering how he could imagine anybody would be cold in the pleasant, scented warmth of the island night.

'No, I'm not cold.' She smiled and added, 'Just an odd shiver . . . like a ghost walking over my grave.'

He nodded gravely, quite as if he was acquainted with some of the more novel expressions of the English language.

'Yes, they are strange sometimes, these premonitions. They can be so certain.'

Did he himself have a premonition? Laurel wondered. She saw Barbie dancing in the arms of the tall, fair man. What was his name – Paul Brenton? Did Manoel have some doubt as he looked at them? Barbie's expression was animated and yet shy at the same time. Laurel, although she had met the younger girl only a short time, had come to know her quite well. She had never seen her look quite like this before, but she knew what it was. It was in just this way that some of the infatuated men who followed the butterfly Anthea around looked when they had danced with her.

Laurel knew a quick sensation of dismay. Barbie had been a tomboy and she still struggled to escape the bonds of a social life, but there had always been latent femininity under the derisive remarks about romance and men in general, a warm heart that waited for the man who would take no notice of such remarks and awaken in her the love that she scorned. Paul Brenton was not that man. He must not be that man.

Knowing so little about him, Laurel still felt that her swift decision was the correct one. Barbie was too inexperienced to recognize the deliberate charm of a man who sought only the light philandery of a passing whim. Laurel knew herself to be little better than Barbie when it came to knowledge of men, but at least she could recognize the type that Paul Brenton represented. Easy and shallow, he would glide through life, hurting those who believed in him and never being hurt himself.

Quite a character reading, Miss Laurel Shannon, she told herself with some amusement.

Her glance went to them again and she saw the man smiling down at the young girl in his arms. His expression was easy to read, while Laurel was gripped by the queerly analytic mood that had descended on her. He was bored with the sophisticated women he knew so well and who played the dangerous game of love as well as he did himself. They knew all the rules and all the answers. He could predict their actions and there was now no longer any interest. Barbie, with her total inexperience, intrigued him.

She did not know that Manoel had followed the direction of her glance until he spoke.

'You have known Barbie for long?'

Laurel brought her attention back to him and shook her head, realizing with a sense of shock that it was only this morning she had met Barbie for the first time.

'I only met her this morning,' she admitted.

'But you are friends?'

'I think so. I hope so anyway,' she added.

'She is so very much without ceremony.'

Laurel flashed him a quick glance, then her eyes went to the couple who were at the other end of the room by now.

Was he thinking of all those times he had encountered the looks of those who wished to attract him and comparing them with Barbie's transparent uninterest in catching any man for a husband – and had he also read correctly the signs of dawning infatuation on Barbie's young face?

She did not know that her glance had returned to him with quite open speculation until his voice brought a quick rush of colour to her face.

'So you have guessed, senhorita?'

Laurel bit her lips in some confusion. 'I . . . I don't . . .' she began, but Manoel shook his head with a faint smile.

'I have no hesitation in admitting it, especially to you who have felt the same thing.'

She wondered for a moment what he was talking about and then remembered that she was supposed to have fallen in love with Stephen the first day she met him – when instead she had just about hated the sight of him.

'Well, I did wonder,' she said after a moment, then gave him a very candid glance. 'Barbie doesn't have much time for men, you know – in a romantic way, I mean.'

Manoel nodded. 'That I had guessed already.' He smiled again in his boyish, charming manner, 'It is perhaps a warning for me to . . . to step lightly.'

In that moment Laurel felt she could quite understand Anthea's penchant for matchmaking – even though her thoughts about that young lady were at the moment rather on the grim side. Manoel was so very likeable and that creature Paul Brenton, with his synthetic smile that seemed to convey the impression that Barbie was the one girl he was looking for, was just the opposite. With it becoming quite obvious to her that Barbie was fast falling from her self-set standard of disdaining men and coming under the spell of that air of worldly charm, whatever failings it might conceal – and there were probably quite a few – she felt a definite desire to interfere herself. Anthea probably would not be able to resist the desire to do so somehow or the other to prevent Barbie from making a fool of herself with a man who was only amusing himself – unless the rashness of her latest escapade – and that was really a very mild word for what she had done – subdued that ebullient spirit of hers, although for the moment, at least on the surface, it did not seem to have had any effect. All the evening she was like a spark of gaiety, but Laurel noticed that never once did she dance with her brother, a manoeuvre that Stephen appeared to make no effort to circumvent. He probably was saving everything he had to say to Anthea for the moment when they were completely alone. She felt quite glad she was not in Anthea's shoes at the moment.

When the time eventually came for the party to break up she determinedly sought Anthea's glance, although her tone was quite casual when she spoke.

'Don't forget I shall be expecting you for lunch to-morrow, Anthea.'

Anthea shook her head. 'As if I could forget!' she replied lightheartedly, quite as if she had not a care in the world.

'I'll probably be bringing her over,' Stephen added, as casually as Laurel had spoken.

'Quite the attentive fiancé,' Roberta murmered with a smile. 'But then you always were attentive, weren't you, Stephen?'

The amused, sympathetic tone did not deceive Laurel in the least. She saw the icy gleam in the elder woman's eyes, almost imperceptible, it was true, but quite definitely there. Perhaps she was the only one who saw it, yet she was quite sure it was not imagination, especially with the meaning that had lain hidden behind those few words.

'Who wouldn't be attentive if Laurel was the girl concerned?' Stephen retorted, with what his supposed fiancée thought was an extremely well acted glance of affection, and she was surprised to find herself feeling grateful to him for it, because Roberta's beauty and sophistication had such a dampening effect on her. She could not see how any man, if he had fallen a victim to it, could ever properly recover.

An odd little silence fell and then, with a feeling of breathless horror, she realized that everyone expected Stephen to kiss her goodnight, before Ned drove Barbie and herself home.

'Sorry, but it seems inevitable,' he whispered as he took her into his arms.

She knew a moment of sheer panic as he bent his black head down to her, but before she could do anything out of character such as trying to turn her head aside, his mouth was on hers, teasing and almost provocative, making her actually want him to kiss her; and that it seemed was what he had been aiming at, for the next moment he was kissing her altogether differently and her tremulous lips, parted by the insistence of his, were quite unable to do anything but respond. At first she was indignant at being coerced into such a flagrant betrayal of everything she had said about him, then with a sinking heart she realized what had really happened.

She had fallen in love with Stephen Barrington and there was not a thing she could do about it.

CHAPTER FIVE

LAUREL awoke with the feeling that she had done something quite irretrievable, but for a brief moment, until full comprehension returned to her sleep-befuddled senses, she could not think what it was – then she remembered and sat bolt upright in consternation.

Stephen!

It all rushed back in a quite overwhelming flood as she remembered a man's lips on her own, faintly provocative, as if he smiled while he kissed her, belying the mock apology he had made only a moment before. It would be just like Stephen to see the absurd humour of the situation. He had not been smiling the second time he kissed her, though. It had been that kiss which had been her downfall, collapsing all her defences without the least bit of preparation beforehand; and when he had at last lifted his head, he had murmured, so softly that only she heard him:

'Tell me after that that you hate me and I'll call you a liar!'

She had not had the courage to look at him, because she had no doubt whatsoever that she would have met a completely unrepentant grin that dared her to deny that she had enjoyed it.

Enjoyed it? That was about the silliest, most tame description that could have been applied to such an experience. After the first shocked indignation she had felt as if she had been drawn without warning into a living electric current. It had hit her with such shattering force that for one crazy moment she had almost been lost enough to sink down into complete, enchanted bewitchment. It had only been the fact that in one split second she had realized what had happened to her that had enabled her to make a snatch at her reeling self-control. She did not have a hope of pretending in future that she disliked his kisses, but at least she had managed to hide from him the full extent to which she had been affected.

A little shiver of pure horror went through her at the thought of how very nearly she had betrayed herself. On Stephen's side it had probably been caused largely by the memory of her remark while they were dancing that if she had to be kissed she did not see why she should not enjoy it, coupled with the fact that he had an audience to play up to.

On her own side, though, it was not something that could be passed off as a momentary weakness. Sleeping on her discovery of the night before had not made the slightest difference. It had not been the least bit of good telling herself, before she dropped off to sleep, that she could not have chosen a more unlikely man to fall in love with, that the whole thing was quite impossible and would only cause her a lot of unhappiness. The fact remained that, when she awoke in the morning, she found out quite definitely that, whether she liked it or not, she was still in love with Stephen Barrington – and she was quite sure that she did not like the idea, because it was one of those dead-end avenues with heartbreak at the end of it.

She swung her legs out of bed with a fervent prayer that Stephen had not had the least inkling last night of just what his kisses had done to her. If he was still unsuspicious she only had to take good care in future that he remained that way, but if he had received the slightest hint that she was by no means impervious to his attraction as she made out, the impossible situation they were in would become all the more unbearable, for herself at least. She had no doubt that Stephen himself would be able to carry it off with his usual self-possession and *savoir faire*, but every time she saw him she would feel like crawling into a dark hole in the ground and curling up into a miserable little bundle, hoping that the heavens would fall and hide her abject humiliation, especially after some of the things she had said to him.

Apart from all other considerations, she was disgusted with herself for allowing it to happen. The only thing that helped was that it had apparently crept up on her unawares and people did say that, even if its onslaught was recognized, there was no defence against love. It was just one of those things over which human beings had no control, even though some of them might have to hide it, when the little laughing god had reduced them to unconditional surrender. She was, in a way, a little stunned by the discovery that she had ended up by loving a man she had been quite sure she disliked only a few days ago. Even yesterday there had been moments when she had felt the desire to hit him – very hard. He would probably annoy her again and again in the future, but that would not alter the fact of her love for him.

And, of course, there was Roberta Fransom.

She busied herself getting ready for Anthea's projected visit in the hope that it would keep at bay thoughts that had become painful as well as humiliating with the introduction of Roberta into them, but it did not help much. She still found herself wondering how much Stephen had loved the beautiful red-haired woman and whether Roberta still had the power to weave a spell over him, the ability to bring him back to her a willing slave to an attraction he could not fight.

Once she had believed he was incapable of loving anyone, but now she was not so sure. She had a swift flash of memory, seeing him again as he had stood on the terrace at Castelanto, the mockery erased from his dark face for one instant of time, leaving it stark and lonely, before he quickly eased the mask back into place. It must have been Roberta, the memory of what she had done to him, that had brought the expression of bitterness to his face, remembered pain that the years had not quite been able to erase – and if she had hurt him once, she would do so again, because no woman could hurt a man in such a manner if she truly loved him.

For the first time she began to be glad of her fake engagement, because it seemed some measure of protection against the beautiful Roberta, for how long she did not know. She was fiercely determined that Stephen should not be hurt any more if she could prevent it, although how she could possibly have any power to do so was beyond her. Even though it was quite stupid, she still felt the desire to protect him, knowing that it was the last thing in the world he would allow or desire. She was able to conjure up too easily a quite, painfully accurate vision of the jeering derision his face would wear if he guessed she was harbouring such ideas.

Probably her desire to protect him was rather ridiculous. Stephen Barrington was quite capable of taking care of himself. If he still felt attracted to Roberta, he would doubtless weigh up what she was and assess that against his desire for her, knowing that this time she must have some genuine affection for him, because she was rich in her own right now.

She sighed and shook her head, because it all seemed quite beyond her. The only thing she was sure of was that falling in love with Stephen Barrington was the last thing she should have done.

Over breakfast Ned teased her about her engagement and Laurel found it surprisingly easy to keep up the pretence. She wanted to tell him just what had happened, but she decided not to do so, because she knew that Stephen would not want anyone to know what had prompted Anthea's amazing announcement, and she could not tell Ned that the engagement was a fake without also informing him of the reason for it.

Anthea arrived at lunchtime, looking somewhat subdued and accompanied by Stephen. Laurel felt her heart give a little lurch she was quite unable to control, because so suddenly he had come to mean more to her than she had ever dreamed he could.

Lunch went off lightheartedly. Stephen was the perfect example of the teasing, affectionate fiancé, and although Laurel tried hard to detect any sign that he might have realized what had happened to her last night, there was not the least hint of it. The danger of that might be when they were alone and she was glad that moment was to be postponed for some little time yet.

Immediately after lunch Ned took Stephen off somewhere around the plantation, but Laurel was quite sure that the idea was not his, although the suggestion had certainly come from him. Stephen was just as adroit as his sister when it came to manoeuvring people. He knew quite well that she would want to speak to Anthea alone and he was more than a match for his sister had she shown any desire to postpone the moment of explanation. Anthea, however, made no attempt to try to outwit him.

She leaned back in her chair, a ghost of her old, irrepressible smile on her lips, but at the same time there was something tense about her attitude. She was defiant and challenging, as if she realized the enormity of what she had done, but still did not regret it in the least.

'Well?' she said, with just a faint tinge of trepidation in her voice. 'You might as well let fly. I'm used to it by now. Stephen has already wiped the floor with me.'

Laurel made a hopeless little gesture with one hand. 'Why on earth did you do it?'

Anthea dropped her gaze. For one moment her composure seemed to break. She looked young and defenceless and when she glanced up her eyes were quite unshielded.

'I told you once that I would do anything to stop Stephen being hurt again, and ... and I was desperate.'

'Roberta Fransom was the woman he was engaged to before?'

Anthea nodded, showing no surprise that Laurel had heard of her brother's previous engagement.

'It was stupid, I suppose,' she admitted, 'but I challenged her outright with coming to Ladrana to try to get Stephen back and she admitted it. I ... I think I went a little crazy for a moment.' Her great blue eyes pleaded for understanding and she bit her lip almost fiercely as she went on. 'I didn't know how Stephen felt about her, but I was sure she would never make him happy, after the way she had acted when they'd been engaged before.' She paused again and then added quietly, 'If you can bear with me for a moment I think I'd better tell you just what did happen, then you may be able to understand why I acted like I did.'

'All right,' Laurel agreed, just as quietly.

'It happened some years ago. Stephen had gone to England on holiday. I was at school there at the time and the first time he came to visit me we had a wonderful time together. He was altogether different then, not cynical, a little wild, I suppose. All the older girls at school fell head over heels in love with him at first sight and I just basked in the glory of having him there. I absolutely adored him and . . . . I suppose I still do, even though he's changed such a lot,' she added in a low voice. 'Then after a little while he didn't come to see me so frequently and one day he brought Roberta with him. I suppose I was a little jealous, but I honestly tried to like her, for Stephen's sake. I called myself all sorts of names, telling myself that I was just jealous and horrible, but I couldn't like her, however much I tried. Stephen was crazy about her, but I seemed to know somehow that she was not sincere, perhaps because I loved him so much myself.'

She shrugged. 'Anyway, they became engaged and Stephen was just walking on air. Young as I was, I was afraid for him – then the crash came.' She broke off again and twisted the fragile handkerchief she held. 'A rather bad storm struck one of the islands a little further north. It had a name very much like Ladrana. You know how garbled these things can become. It wasn't important enough to merit an official news item, but it managed to find its way back to England somehow or the other and Roberta eventually received a twisted version that said Ladrana had been hit by a hurricane, everything completely flattened on the island and everyone there ruined.' She made a contemptuous little gesture, her eyes hard. 'Even if it had been true, it would have taken far more than that to ruin Stephen.' Her lips twisted bitterly, with the same contempt that had been in her gesture a moment ago. 'Most gold-diggers are thorough, but apparently Roberta wasn't too well versed in her "career" – she was very young then – and she thought that the estates on Ladrana were all that Stephen owned. She was a bit of a coward, too, because she didn't stop to find out from Stephen himself whether he really had been ruined by this supposed hurricane. Perhaps she loved him as much as she's capable of loving anyone besides herself and thought he might persuade her to marry him, even if he didn't have any money. The first intimation Stephen had that it was his money she had wanted and not so much himself was when he saw a notice in the paper that she had married someone else by special licence.'

'How awful for him,' Laurel said softly, as Anthea paused. Her eyes were darkened with pain, as if she shared the hurt bewilderment and disillusion that must have struck so deeply at the man she loved.

Anthea's soft lips hardened again. 'I always felt it would have been far worse if she had married him and he had found out afterwards what she was like.' She leaned forward suddenly and caught Laurel's hands in her own. 'She wants him back now – and that's the last thing that must happen.'

'But suppose Stephen still loves her .., that Roberta loves him. . . . ?'

'Roberta is quite incapable of loving anyone but herself,' Anthea retorted, with such scorn in her young voice that Laurel found herself unable to do anything but agree.

'She must have some affection for him to try and get him back,' she pointed out, still putting up a fight, even though she thoroughly agreed with Anthea without the necessity of persuasion. 'After all, she has money of her own now. Quite apart from putting both Stephen and myself in an embarrassing position, you should have given him a chance to make up his own mind what he was going to do. If he still loves her, it will be with his eyes open to what she is.'

'Then you don't like her either!' Anthea sounded triumphant and satisfied, but she quickly became earnest again, her hands adding their own mute pleading to her words. 'Oh, Laurel, can't you see that she mustn't have him back? She's shallow and selfish. Stephen deserves far better.'

In spite of herself, Laurel could not help a little thrill of pleasure that Anthea should think she was suited to the brother she adored, but it did not alter the complete certainty she felt that, left to himself, she would have been the last person Stephen would have chosen to become engaged to and no doubt he would heave a heartfelt sigh of relief when this mock engagement came to an end. On the other hand, she fully agreed with Anthea that Roberta was not the woman he should marry. No woman who had ever thrown over a man for purely selfish reasons, as Roberta's desire for a wealthy husband had been, could ever be trusted with his happiness again.

'Yes, he does deserve better,' she said slowly, hardly aware that she had spoken aloud until Anthea's fingers gripped hard on her own again.

'I know you hate me getting my sticky fingers into other people's business,' she pleaded earnestly, 'but this time even you must admit that it was justified – although I suppose I did go to extremes,' she added with a wry little grimace at what Laurel privately thought went beyond a mere extreme. 'It was all I could think of on the spur of the moment. I just had to do something to stop Roberta getting her claws into him again!'

'You can't stop her if Stephen decides he wants her back,' Laurel pointed out with irrefutable truth. 'This engagement will naturally not last very long, just time enough for the nine days' wonder to die down. It was Stephen's own suggestion that I should begin to show interest in someone else after a time, so that nobody will be particularly surprised when the engagement is broken. It flared up so suddenly they probably don't expect it to last in any event.'

Anthea gave a little grunt that could have signified anything. She scowled at the blank wall for a moment, then directed her gloomy frown at Laurel.

'I'm beginning to wish I'd picked on somebody who at least liked Stephen,' she muttered disgustedly, making Laurel feel that she had been switched somehow to the position of defendant instead of Anthea. 'They might have been agreeable to do something about the Roberta problem.'

'What can be done about her?' Laurel asked involuntarily, with an uneasy feeling the next moment that she may have somehow involved herself even deeper in the matter by her seemingly innocent question.

Anthea gave her a glance of scorn. 'If you had half an ounce of feminine guile you wouldn't need to ask that.'

'Are you suggesting that I should compete with Roberta?' She managed to keep her voice coolly amused, but only with an effort, because she suspected that it was just that course of action Anthea was advocating.

'And why not?'

She smiled, as if the answer was quite obvious. 'Because I wouldn't stand a chance against her – even if I was willing to try,' she added hastily, before Anthea could take her reply as any sort of submission to her absurd demand.

Anthea made an impatient movement. 'I don't see why you shouldn't have a chance. At least you could try. You played your part effectively enough last night, so you can't dislike him quite as much as you make out.'

'I admit that I don't dislike him as much as I once did,' she said carefully, feeling that even that statement might be a dangerous confidence where Anthea was concerned.

The younger girl's eyes narrowed suddenly in a way that reminded Laurel too sharply and uncomfortably of Stephen.

'You're in love with him,' she said deliberately.

Laurel controlled the involuntary start that the words provoked, but some evidence of her dismay must have shown in her face, because Anthea smiled in a way that was almost cruel.

'You'll do it now,' she said, and her voice was very soft and slow. 'If you love him, you'll fight for him.'

'I don't love him.' Even to her own ears, though she thought that her voice sounded weak and ineffectual. Anthea did not even bother to argue with her over the transparent falsity of the statement.

'If I loved a man, I would want to do everything I could for his happiness.'

'Would you?' Laurel retorted a little bitterly. 'I think you Barringtons have a different idea of love from what I have.'

'Probably,' Anthea agreed, with a hard line to her normally soft lips that heightened her resemblance to Stephen in that moment. 'But not in the way you imagine. I'll grant you that, in your eyes, we probably seem to racket around a bit, but it's harmless enough, and when I do fall in love I know that it will be the end of everything else. Stephen is the same. It's a trait that runs in the family.'

'Is it?' Laurel tried to sound indifferent and knew she was not succeeding too well.

'It is. If I was in your position I would fight tooth and nail for him. At least we know how to love,' she said scornfully. 'It's probably come down from old Dom Miguel. But your love can't be worth much if you just want to crawl into a hole and let Roberta get away with everything.'

Laurel winced, but she could not find any words to refute the statement that was only partly true. She was very much on the defensive now, when only a short time ago it had been Anthea in that position. There had been a complete reversal, which only a Barrington could have effected in such a manner.

Anthea abruptly changed her tactics. Her expression softened. She smiled wistfully.

'Don't you think he's worth fighting for?'

Whether the tone was deliberately assumed or not, the choice of words broke down her resistance more than anything else could have done.

'Yes . . . yes, he is worth fighting for,' she whispered. He was worth anything. She knew that only too well.

Anthea's eyes narrowed. There was triumph in them now. 'Then you'll do it?'

Laurel looked at her bitterly. 'You Barringtons have no scruples about manoeuvring people just as you want them, have you?'

'You will do it?' Anthea insisted.

Laurel nodded and went down into complete defeat. 'Yes, I will do it – although I know that I haven't a chance of success against Roberta.'

Anthea laughed gaily, fully restored in an instant to all her old charm and airy whimsicality.

'Don't be so downhearted.' She flicked back a strand of blonde hair. 'Stephen was right. You do need some lessons on how to handle men.'

'Perhaps I do,' Laurel agreed grimly, 'but I'll handle this in my own way.'

Just how was she going to handle the impossible and rather frightening matter of trying to make Stephen Barrington fall in love with her? She had not the faintest idea how to go about it and the greatest reluctance in the world to even begin.

When they went out into the garden Stephen and Ned seemed to be on their way back to meet them. Anthea immediately went across and thrust her arm through Ned's with a gamin smile up at him.

'How do, brother Ned,' she said gaily. 'What do you think of your new sister-to-be?'

'Really want me to tell you?' Ned countered, and Laurel saw a swift flash of pain cross her brother's face before he recovered himself. Knowing his feelings were far from brotherly towards the lovely fair-headed girl at his side, Laurel only just stopped herself putting out a hand to her brother in a rush of sympathy, because she knew just what it was like now to be in love with somebody who would probably be quite willing to have a light and meaningless affair with you but did not care a jot seriously. In her own case she did not know whether Stephen would have been interested even in that. He had once said – on a very momentous and well remembered occasion – that he liked his women sophisticated and experienced, and she was neither. Besides, Roberta Fransom had appeared on the scene now.

She felt him come up behind her and his arms slid around her waist, drawing her back against him. Just for one moment, she stiffened, then slowly relaxed, leaning her head back against his hard chest. Over her head Stephen looked across at his sister with a dryly quizzical glance. From her he shifted his gaze to Ned.

'You'd better not tell her the truth, Ned. She'd never stand it this afternoon.'

Anthea pouted and darted a sorry little glance up at the tow-headed man at her side.

'You'll simply have to be nice to me, Ned darling. They've both been flaying me alive.'

'For letting the cat out of the bag, you mean?' Ned asked. 'Serves you right,' he added unsympathetically.

Anthea pouted, but she nevertheless looked a little piqued. Her glance became speculative and she gnawed at her lower lip in a manner that her own brother had come to realize meant she was embarking on something or considering some idea that she should never have entertained in the first place.

'I don't think the cat was very securely in the bag in any case,' she retorted.

'Well, you should know,' Stephen countered softly, while Laurel simply stood in the circle of his arms, not saying a word, just savouring the bitter-sweet pleasure of being so near to him without having to pretend that she was completely indifferent. She silently blessed Ned for being a one-man audience. Had only Anthea been present there would have been no need for pretence and she would have had to free herself from Stephen, in case he guessed how every nerve was thrilling and singing at his touch. In that moment she felt quite blissfully happy and refused to think about Roberta.

She saw Ned grin at her and knew exactly what he was thinking. He had apparently always liked Stephen Barrington and was thoroughly satisfied with his sister's choice of a marriage partner. Well, he would soon learn differently, she thought with a shade of grimness. The Stephen Barringtons of this world did not pick on inexperienced little schoolteachers without an ounce of glamour or distinction.

The thought caused her a little twinge of pain she could not control and the bitter-sweet pleasure of Stephen's arms around her became more pain than anything else, so that she could not bear him to touch her in that moment.

Carefully she relaxed the fingers of one hand until the handkerchief she had been clutching in it fluttered down to the ground. Using it as an excuse to free herself, she bent to pick it up and then moved a few feet away, to perch on a low, ornamental wall, swinging one foot with an appearance of casual composure, whatever Anthea might thing of her actions – or Stephen too for that matter.

She was trying to think of some safe, casual topic – as casual as she hoped her expression was – to swing the conversation around to, but Pepita appeared at the back door of the house and came towards them, making it unnecessary.

As she slid down off the wall and advanced to meet the Portuguese woman she had to pass Stephen. A certain sardonic amusement in his expression, that Ned could not see, told her that he realized she had found the moment awkward for some reason, even if he did not know what had caused it – at least she hoped with all her heart that he did not know. It did not need his softly uttered remark, so low that only she heard it:

'Saved by the gong!'

She hoped she was keeping her expression appropriately undisturbed, and then Pepita was bobbing her funny little curtsey and announcing:

'The Senhora Bertram-Smythe, she is here.'

'Oh, lord!' Anthea groaned.

'We'll be coming in now,' Laurel said quickly, to cover up Anthea's involuntary but rather unfortunate exclamation. She did not know yet how much Pepita was to be trusted not to gossip.

'I tell her,' Pepita nodded, and scuttled off ahead of them.

Ned grinned after her. 'Mama B-S has probably come to black her nose about your engagement,' he said with a glance at Stephen, who merely shrugged.

'It's probably all over the island by now.'

As they entered the house, Laurel felt him catch her hand and grip her fingers rather hard, both for appearance and also in warning.

'Come on, play up, you little coward,' he whispered, and because Laurel felt that was just about adding insult to injury she tipped up her head with a reckless laugh that dared him to call her a coward when the whole situation had been caused by a Barrington in the first place.

'Darling Stephen, anything you say,' she said gaily, loud enough for Mrs. Bertram-Smythe, just on the other side of the doorway they approached, to hear her.

'Anything?' Stephen countered, doubtless for the same reason.

When they entered the room together, Ned and Anthea following close behind them, they must have looked the typical happily engaged couple. Mrs. Bertram-Smythe rose to her feet and held out both her hands to them with an affected gesture, which gave Laurel the opportunity to free her hands from Stephen's clasp.

'So it is true after all!' She directed a playfully coy glance at Stephen. 'You dark horse, Stephen Barrington. Annexing Laurel for yourself the first moment she appeared on the island!'

'Who wouldn't?' Stephen answered, with what his fiancée thought would have been quite touching gallantry if he had really meant it.

'I was so surprised when I heard,' Mrs. Bertram-Smythe gushed on, 'but of course I knew it was true the moment I saw you. You both look so happy. I don't know how you managed to hide it so completely before.'

'Well, it was rather hard,' Stephen agreed equably, while out of the corner of her eye Laurel saw that Anthea's lovely face was positively wreathed in gleeful amusement, which she hastily erased as Barbie's mother brought her attention to the second member of the un-accountable Barrington family.

'And what do you think of it, Anthea dear?'

'Oh, I'm positively delighted,' Anthea told her, speaking what was probably nothing but the blatant, unadorned truth. 'It's what I wanted right from the beginning.'

'Did you?' Stephen murmured, and just for one moment his eyes flickered from his sister to the girl at his side, so that Laurel had a horrible suspicion he was remembering their conversation on the terrace at Castelanto, when he had tried to find out who was involved in Anthea's matchmaking plans.

'I suppose this means you will not be going on with our little plan after all?' Mrs. Bertram-Smythe inquired. 'About the dancing, I mean. I expect you'll be far too busy now. If I know Stephen at all, I'm sure he won't want to let you out of his sight for long, in case somebody else tries to ... er ... poach on his preserves,' she finished roguishly, and Laurel perceived that her worth had gone up considerably in madam's estimation by her astonishing capture of the greatest catch on the island, or the surrounding territory for some distance come to that.

Stephen grinned. 'I'd challenge them to a duel if they tried.' He directed an inquiring glance at his fiancée. 'What dancing plan is this that you've been hatching behind my back?' quite as if he had all the right in the world to know everything that she did.

'Oh, hasn't she told you?' Mrs. Bertram-Smythe asked interestedly.

'No, she hasn't – but we've had quite a lot to talk about lately, haven't we, darling?

Laurel deemed it wiser not to meet Stephen's glance at that moment. 'Quite a lot,' she agreed hastily, but kept her eyes on Mrs. Bertram-Smythe. 'Of course I shall still be going on with it,' she added.

Mrs. Bertram-Smythe gave a nod of satisfaction, refused an invitation to join them for refreshments and began to pull on her gloves.

'I should love to stay,' she excused herself, 'but it's so unfortunate. I have a meeting this afternoon. I just dropped in on my way, so that I could tell the ladies whether you would be going on with our little plan.'

'Just dropped by!' Anthea grimaced, when Mrs. Bertram-Smythe had taken her departure and the only trace that remained of her visit was a cloud of dust from her car disappearing in the distance. 'It's quite a bit out of her way to come here before going to Milton, the old news bulletin!' She grinned at Laurel. 'If you ever want to spread anything around the island, just drop a hint to Mrs. B-S. If you hint that it's top secret and for her ears alone she'll do a quicker job still.' She studied the other girl with bright, dancing eyes. 'Anyway, what is all this about some sort of a dance?'

'She stands on one foot, touches her toes backwards and points the other foot at the lampshade,' Ned grinned.

'Quite an effort.' Stephen quirked one of those diabolical black eyebrows. 'Are you going to give us an exhibition, darling?' he inquired of his fiancée.

'Ned is exaggerating,' Laurel said calmly. 'I used to belong to a physical culture organization that specialized in classical Greek dancing.' Before he could make one of the remarks that so easily sent the colour flying to her cheeks, she launched quickly into the explanation she had given Mrs. Dalkeith and the secretary of Milton's ladies' club. 'I want something to occupy my time,' she added in explanation. 'It seemed a good idea, to combine it with a kindergarten school.'

Anthea grimaced. 'Must you have the school, too? I can't imagine you bossing a lot of kids.'

'Nor can I,' Stephen murmured, with his grey glance flicking over her from head to foot, and, because she had an idea of what was coming, Laurel forestalled him.

'Don't you think that joke is getting a little stale?' she asked. 'Whatever you think about it, I was a schoolteacher and I doubtless shall be one again.'

'Haven't you forgotten something, my child?' Stephen drawled. 'You're going to be married. I shall demand too much of your time for you to start playing at school-teachers again.'

Quite apart from the fact that she should not have slipped into the unguarded remark about going back to schoolteaching one day, Laurel was annoyed with him, because he knew quite well, as did Anthea and herself, that the engagement between them would never lead to marriage. She had known it was going to hurt, but never quite as much as this. She wanted to hit back at him, but it was impossible to do so too pointedly with Ned present, so instead she smiled.

'Well, perhaps the kindergarten wouldn't be such a good idea at the moment, but as I don't intend to give up all my time to you, my dear husband-to-be, I shall go on with my Greek dancing if I can get enough people interested,' which would show Stephen quite plainly that she was attempting to pay him back in his own coin, but her mock determined attitude would deceive Ned into thinking that she was just joking. He would take it as the remark of a happily engaged girl who really wanted nothing better than to be all the time with the man she loved, but Stephen would be astute enough to see through to the truth and Anthea, who as well as her brother knew the true state of affairs, would also realize that she did not intend to be pushed around too much by the Barringtons. She was quite independent and intended to stand on her own feet. Even though Anthea might know how she felt about her tall, dark-haired brother, Stephen himself did not realize that she would have given any-thing for the right to be always at his side.

'That's telling him!' Anthea murmured, with her eyes dancing. She appeared not at all put out by the oblique warning that Laurel intended to retain her independence whatever the state of her feelings towards Stephen. She directed a sparkling glance at her brother. 'You'd better beat her often when you're married.'

'There are other ways to tame her,' Stephen retorted enigmatically, and Laurel blushed, remembering that first punishing kiss in the gardens at Castelanto. Anthea probably thought of the same method by her expression and Laurel rushed quickly into speech, before the irrepressible Miss Barrington could say something completely outrageous.

'I've already more or less promised, so I would have to go on with the show, even if I didn't want to.' She gave Anthea a restrained glance. 'I thought you might have been interested in taking part in it.'

Anthea chuckled. 'I'd love to, so long as you give me the part of the nymph who's chased by the satyr!'

'Most probably it would end up with the satyr being chased by the nymph,' Ned retorted, at which Anthea wrinkled up her nose at him. 'Or more likely the goddess Venus chasing some unfortunate male.'

'Who said he'd be unfortunate?' Anthea demanded indignantly, and with some surprise Laurel realized that her good-natured, easy-going brother was quite a match for the female half of the Barrington family. Whatever his personal feelings might be, he put up a good front in dealing with his unfortunate love for Anthea. Somewhat intrigued, she wondered if she presented the same undisturbed appearance to Stephen.

It was hard to know the exact impression one made on another person, even though quite a lot could be guessed at. If she could do as well as Ned she would feel a lot safer from Stephen finding out how much he really meant to her, but Anthea knew, and she had an uneasy feeling that the other girl would not hesitate to inform Stephen himself if it suited whatever plan she might be hatching at the time. That did not stop her liking Anthea though, which seemed another effect of the Barrington charm.

Once or twice during the afternoon she noticed Anthea watching her speculatively, with just a hint of exasperation, and wondered what was causing the expression.

She had no need to ask. Anthea had no hesitation in bringing up the subject herself.

The two girls had gone up to Laurel's room, so that Anthea could renew her make-up before she left, and she swung round from the stool set before the dressing-table, pointing her lipstick at Laurel in a way that was oddly reminiscent of the first evening they had met.

'You're not trying nearly hard enough,' she stated positively.

'What do you mean?'

Anthea made an impatient little movement. 'You know as well as I do what I mean. Every time Stephen comes near you, you just freeze up.'

Laurel turned away, looking out of the window. 'I suppose it hasn't occurred to you that I might be afraid of giving myself away?' she asked quietly.

Anthea came across to her side instantly. Her hand caught at Laurel's bare arm in instant contrition. 'I'm sorry, Laurel. I know it must be hard for you, but. ...' She gave a whimsical little smile and added persuasively, 'Don't treat him like a contaminating disease.'

Laurel turned round, a look of surprise and dismay on her face. 'Do I ...? Do I treat him like that?'

Anthea made a deprecating little gesture. 'Well, not as bad as that, I suppose ... but you certainly make it quite plain that you're not keen to have him near you.' She shrugged. 'I don't suppose Ned noticed. He's quite obtuse about that sort of thing and he likes Stephen, so if he did notice he would probably put it down to shyness on your part.'

Laurel looked thoughtful as she picked up a comb to run through the cap of short tobacco-brown curls that clustered all over her head, but there was an eminently satisfied expression on Miss Barrington's face as she went downstairs with her hostess.

Stephen and Ned were waiting for them in the little hallway. Anthea tripped downstairs, gaily swinging her white handbag by its strap, but Laurel followed more slowly. Stephen's powerful maroon car was parked outside. He handed Anthea into the front seat and slammed the door on her impertinent remarks, but she quickly shot down the window and continued to chaff Ned through the opening.

Laurel hesitated a moment, then moved closer to Stephen and lifted her head for the goodbye kiss that would be expected. He grinned and accepted the invitation, expertly and thoroughly, then kissed her again for good measure. She could not quite decide whether she wanted to hit him for his very evident amusement.

'Courage, my child. You'll survive,' he murmured, and then slid into the front seat of the car to start the engine softly purring.

Laurel watched the car receding into the usual cloud of dust and yearned for a miracle to happen.

Barbie was the next visitor to the Shannon ménage. She arrived on the morning following Anthea's dressing down, dusty, hot and with swollen, red-rimmed eyes.

Laurel gave her a glance of dismay. 'Barbie! Whatever has happened?'

Barbie bit her lips and seemed to be on the verge of more tears. 'I've had a row with Mother,' she muttered finally.

Ned chose that moment to show up in the doorway, but Laurel signalled to him silently to leave her alone with Barbie. He took one look at the miserable Barbie, who had bowed her head in her hands and consequently had not seen him enter, nodded understandingly and disappeared.

Laurel sat down on the couch at the younger girl's side and gently but determinedly drew her hands down from her face.

'Now, suppose you tell me what happened,' she said quietly. She was just a little surprised that Barbie should have come to her in her distress, rather than gone to Anthea, who she had known longer.

Barbie made a pettish little movement. 'Oh, it's Mother! Always wanting to marry me off to someone!'

Laurel smiled, but hastily erased it. 'Who is it this time? Manoel?'

Barbie nodded. She looked up, her eyes still bright with tears. 'I feel so humiliated. We were in Milton . . . I hoped she hadn't seen him, but of course she had. She was all over him in no time and . . . and it was so obvious. I don't know what he must be thinking now.'

Laurel had a good idea what he was probably thinking, since if he had his way he would be a willing catch in Mrs. Bertram-Smythe's too obvious net.

'I'm sure he didn't think anything of it,' she suggested soothingly.

'But he must have,' Barbie insisted. 'I know Mother means well, but she makes me feel awful sometimes. Besides . . . besides, I'm in love with someone else,' she added in a hesitant whisper.

This time Laurel felt real consternation, because she could guess only too well who had become the recipient of Barbie's young, inexperienced heart. The girl had avoided men so much she simply had no idea how to tell the difference between the experienced, blasé philanderer and sincere affection.

'Congratulations,' she said with a smile, hiding her dismay as best she could and finding that her experience of hiding her true feelings from Stephen had made her quite expert at it. 'This is rather a reversal of opinion after the scathing denouncement of men only a few days ago. Who is responsible for it?'

'Paul Brenton,' Barbie said, and blushed.

'But you only met him two days ago,' Laurel attempted to point out. 'How can you be so sure?'

'You fell in love with Stephen the first day you met him,' Barbie said triumphantly, and Laurel accorded her a silent salute, finding herself hoist with her own petard, or rather one of Stephen's fabrications.

'Yes, I suppose I did,' she admitted. 'But you don't

125

know anything about him really, do you?'

Barbie waved her tentative warning aside. 'I know all I need to know about him, that I love him and that he loves me.'

Heavens, the man was a quick worker! Laurel felt her dismay rise sharply, because she was quite certain that, even from her limited experience of him, Paul Brenton felt nothing of the kind. Whatever attraction Barbie had for him, there was little doubt that it went no further than the attraction of novelty. When the newness wore off he would have no qualms about leaving her. If she gave way to what could only be infatuation, Barbie was just laying herself open to heartbreak and disillusionment possibly even danger. She had a horrible suspicion that Paul Brenton was the type of man who would not even respect Barbie's total innocence of men. However, no good would come of trying to dissuade her outright. It would only make her all the more determined. There was a lot of child in Barbie still and luckily Laurel knew just how to deal with children.

'Well, I suppose you know your own mind best,' she said briskly, as she rose to her feet. 'The main problem at the moment seems to be your mother's intentions to pair you off with Manoel. Suppose we get that settled first?'

Barbie gave her a look of trusting confidence. 'What can we do about it? She'll only give up when he becomes engaged to somebody else. I suppose there's no chance of that?' she added hopefully.

Laurel shook her head. 'Not that I know of.' Anthea had more or less admitted that he was quite free and did not have any entanglements that she knew of, and Anthea's knowledge of such matters was usually quite extensive. 'I suppose you couldn't pretend to your mother that he is interested in someone else,' she suggested.

Barbie shook her head instantly. 'Not a hope. That would only make her work quicker – and more obviously,' she added gloomily.

'There's only one thing for it, then – we'll have to explain the whole matter to Manoel himself.'

Barbie's eyes opened wide in horror. 'I couldn't!' she gasped. 'I feel bad enough about it as it is.'

Laurel smiled down at her. 'I was not suggesting that you should do the explaining. I'll speak to him for you, if you like.'

Barbie brightened up instantly. 'Oh, would you?' The next moment she looked a bit doubtful. 'He'll probably think it rather strange.'

'I doubt it.' She handed Barbie her own handkerchief as the younger girl seemed to be hunting helplessly for something to dry her eyes with. 'Don't forget he comes from an environment where parents often arrange their children's marriages. This sort of thing must happen quite often, the parents wanting their daughter to marry some particular man and the girl having entirely different ideas about who she wants to marry. He'll probably think it's quite romantic and want to help you.'

If the help included throwing Barbie into Paul Brenton's arms, she knew that would be the last thing Manoel de Valente would desire, but between them they could probably circumvent such an unwelcome climax. For a moment it occurred to her that she might have appealed to Stephen for help of some kind, but she dismissed it almost immediately. There was little that he could do and, in any case, it was Manoel's right to give any help that was needed, as he loved Barbie.

She left Barbie mopping up her eyes and went into the kitchen, where Ned was hovering around anxiously, having dismissed Pepita out to the region of the kitchen garden. He had already put the kettle on.

'I'm making some tea,' he almost whispered, as if his voice could reach Barbie. 'That will make her feel better.'

Laurel smiled at his assumption that tea was the cure for everything, even love affairs.

'Thanks, Ned.'

'What's the matter with her, anyway?'

'Just that matchmaking mother of hers.' She hesitated a moment, then decided to tell Ned everything she knew.

He whistled softly when she finished. 'Paul Brenton! I've heard of him.' He glanced at his sister and shook his head. 'He's bad medicine, my pet. We'd better get her out of his clutches if we possibly can.'

'What have you heard about him, then?'

Ned made a deprecating gesture. 'Don't like to gossip,' he said hesitantly, 'but I heard one or two things about him when I was on holiday about a year ago in Lourenço Marques. He apparently lived around there for a time and acquired rather a bad reputation with women. He was mixed up in a particularly unsavoury divorce case at one time. The woman committed suicide afterwards. There was a rumour went round that she was going to have a baby and did it because he refused to marry her.'

'Good heavens!' Laurel sounded startled. She had instinctively felt that Paul Brenton was bad, but her intuition had never led her this far. It now became all the more imperative to free Barbie from an infatuation which could be actually dangerous.

'Want any help?' Ned inquired, as his sister filled a tray and prepared to depart.

'No, I can manage her all right. Do you mind having your tea alone, Ned? I think she'd rather not have an audience to have to play up to. I won't tell her that you know.'

Ned shook his head instantly. 'Of course I don't mind. Just pour me out a cup before you go.' He started to reach for the teapot, then changed his mind. 'No, better still, I'll make myself another pot in this one.'

He hauled a tiny blue china teapot down off the shelf, and Laurel reached up to kiss his cheek affectionately.

'You're a darling, Ned.'

He grinned down at her and slipped his arm around her shoulders to hug her swiftly.

'You're not so bad yourself, Miss Shannon.'

Laurel returned to the lounge to find that Barbie had

recovered enough to feel ashamed of her outburst. She came across the room swiftly and took the tray from the elder girl, and, because she guessed that it helped her, Laurel let her take it and set it down on the table.

'I'm beginning to feel ashamed of myself for bothering you with all my troubles,' she said apologetically.

'Don't be silly,' Laurel retorted. 'You know I'm glad to help.'

'I just didn't think about it ... just came barging in. I felt so upset I ran out of the house and started to walk as fast as I could. I found myself near here when I came to.'

'Just as well that you did,' Laurel told her briskly. 'Everything will work out all right. Don't worry about it. Drink up your tea and then we'll go and see if we can find Manoel.'

'He'll probably be on his yacht. He was going back there when we left him in town this morning.'

'Then we'll go and beard him in his den.' She grimaced. 'I hope I can make his crew understand that I want to see him. I don't know a word of Portuguese.'

'I do. You tend to pick it up on the island, as there are still quite a lot of Portuguese here,' Barbie explained. 'I could come with you, although I would rather not see Manoel myself until you've explained.'

For what Laurel had in mind, she was quite sure she did not want Barbie there, so she shook her head.

'You go home. I'll manage all right.'

Barbie finished her tea in a far happier frame of mind and Laurel then borrowed Ned's car and dropped her off home, prior to going in to Milton. As Barbie stood at the gate of the house, Laurel put her head out of the car window and smiled, leaving the engine still running.

'Don't worry. Everything will be all right. Come to lunch tomorrow and you can find out what happened.'

'Thanks, I'd love to.' She grimaced as Mrs. Bertram-Smythe appeared inquiringly in the doorway. 'I'd better go in now and make my peace with Mother.'

She turned with a wave of one hand that silently conveyed her gratitude and Laurel efficiently put the car in gear and drove off, hoping that if she ever chanced to do so in Stephen's vicinity she would do it just as smoothly, but knew that she would probably do just the opposite from nervousness.

On the smooth road that led to Milton she had plenty of time to think about Barbie's problem and rather welcomed its advent, because it kept her thoughts off Stephen.

As Ned had said, they had to get Barbie out of Paul Brenton's clutches somehow, and although she did not have the faintest idea how to go about it, unlike Anthea's demand that she should make Stephen fall in love with her, she was sure that this problem at least would work out successfully by some means or the other.

The scattered buildings grew closer together and then she found herself quickly in the small town's wide streets that were bordered by lovely flower gardens. The harbour itself was bordered by a wide esplanade where she was able to leave the car and she quickly scanned the boats moored on the sparkling blue water.

It gave her an odd little shock of surprise to find the coastal freighter that had brought her to the island was still there, loading up this time. There was a miscellany of small craft and, right down near the southernmost curve of the harbour, Stephen's own yacht rode the water like a graceful white bird. There were only two other yachts in the harbour. She walked along to the first of them and found that the name on its side proclaimed it to be the *Firebird* – the yacht which had brought Roberta Fransom to the island. With a quick, cold little feeling she passed on to the remaining one, painted white like Stephen's, but with the name *Rosaritos* on its sleek hull, which would have told her it belonged to Manoel, without the confirmation of a burst of conversation from its decks that was quite incomprehensible to her.

She approached the neat little gangway somewhat

tentatively, under a sudden silence from the deck, as the two men lounging at the head of the gangway turned their attention fully on her. One was young and rather attractive, the other grizzled and old, but both were regarding her with quite open admiration that would have made her blush if she had not been amused by it.

'Senhor Manoel de Valente?' She put inquiry into her voice, hoping it would be enough for them to guess that she wanted to know if Manoel was aboard. Both of them burst immediately into voluble Portuguese and she repeated Manoel's name, more firmly this time. Finally she was invited aboard, the older man dismissed the younger one with something that had the sound of a definite order, and escorted her to a deck cabin, still talking, blithely unconcerned that she did not understand a word of what he was saying.

The cabin door opened and Manoel himself appeared in the opening. He looked faintly surprised to see her, but instantly smiled.

'Laurel! This is an unexpected pleasure.'

'I hope you think so after you hear what I have to say,' she retorted, returning his smile.

'I am sure I shall,' he replied with his habitual courtesy. He dismissed the seaman with some instructions in Portuguese, then closed the door and turned back to her. 'Please sit down.'

She complied, looking round the cabin interestedly. There was evidence of wealth everywhere, but it was very tasteful evidence. Because she did not quite know where to begin, she occupied herself for long moments in examining her surroundings.

Manoel leaned against a table and smiled down at her. 'You find my ship interesting?'

'Very.' She smiled herself, but it was a rather rueful one. 'I was just stalling for time, actually, as I don't quite know how to begin.' She paused and then decided to go straight into the matter. 'You see, I've come about Barbie.'

Manoel sat down in a chair opposite her, still smiling,

but his manner had changed indefinably.

'Yes, I saw her myself with her mother this morning.'

Laurel nodded. 'Yes, she told me. That . . . that is one of the things I came about.' She broke off, hesitating whether to say what was in her mind, but for the second time decided it was best to be blunt. 'What you said to me the other night, about Barbie, I mean – did you really mean it?'

'That I fell in love with her that day?'

'Yes.'

'I meant it – and I am still in love with her, if that makes it easier for you,' he added, still smiling.

Laurel gave a sigh of relief. 'It makes it a lot easier. Barbie came to see me this morning. She . . . she was rather upset.'

His smile died instantly. 'There is nothing wrong with her, is there?'

She wanted to assure him that there was nothing wrong, but as Paul Brenton was very definitely wrong for Barbie, she could not do so.

She made a deprecating little movement of one hand. 'You may have noticed that Barbie's mother is very anxious for her to marry – somewhat naturally, I suppose.'

'I had noticed,' Manoel admitted dryly.

'Barbie thought you had. That's what upset her. She hates her mother throwing her at men's heads, as she puts it.'

Manoel laughed softly and said something in Portuguese, with a tender light in his very dark eyes.

'I would like to assure Barbie that I would be very glad to have her thrown at my head, but I think that I must tread very lightly yet.'

Laurel thought of an old adage and mentally altered it to 'devils jump in where angels fear to tread'.

She repeated more or less verbatim her conversation with Barbie and was not surprised when she saw his expression darken at mention of Paul Brenton's name.

He nodded. 'I too have heard of him, in other places

besides Lourenço Marques. I could not quite think where I had seen him before, when I met him at your engagement party, but now I remember.'

'What are we going to do about him, then?'

Manoel frowned. 'It does present a problem. Had this situation arisen in the past, I could either have challenged him to a duel or kidnapped her, neither of which would have really solved anything. Killing the man she thought she loved would not have made her love me.'

Laurel smiled at his wry expression. 'You could still kidnap her, of course.'

He laughed slightly. 'The idea is tempting, I admit. However. . . .' His shrug seemed to indicate that it came a few centuries too late, but not that it would have been altogether out of the question had the era been the right one – which made Laurel wonder which side of the family the buccaneer Nicholas Barrington had received his bride-kidnapping ideas from.

There was an interruption as the seamen came back, this time bearing a tray on which were set out cups, tiny sweet cakes and a silver pot that gave out a pleasantly unfamiliar aroma. He set it down on the table and went quietly out again.

Manoel himself poured her out a cup of steaming liquid and handed it to her with his attractive smile.

'Portuguese chocolate. I hope you like it.'

Laurel sipped tentatively, then nodded. 'Lovely.' She wrinkled her brows thoughtfully. 'I think it might be an idea if I invited you to lunch tomorrow, if you're free to come. Barbie will be there,' she added as inducement.

'Matchmaking?' His dark eyes were twinkling.

Laurel gave a shudder. 'Heaven forbid!'

'I would be a very willing victim, I admit. I shall be very glad to accept your invitation.' He grinned with sudden boyishness. 'I feel like a conspirator.'

He looked so attractive at that moment that she wondered how on earth Barbie could prefer Paul Brenton's rather dissipated, deliberate charm to Manoel de Valente's far higher worth. All in all, she felt quite satisfied with her afternoon when she at last left the yacht to return home. If she could arrange other such meetings Manoel and Barbie would be able to get to know each other without Mrs. Bertram-Smythe's overdone tactics – and then she directed a mental grimace at herself and decided not to be so exasperated with Anthea's own matchmaking *penchant* in future, since she seemed to be more or less guilty of the same thing herself.

If her conscience bothered her at all about interfering, she quietened it with the assurance that Paul Brenton could not possibly be allowed to get away with breaking Barbie's heart, which she was quite sure he would do once the novelty of her had worn off. Barbie was worth a far better fate than that.

When Barbie came to lunch the following day, she bore little resemblance to the dusty, tear-stained object that had confronted Laurel the previous afternoon. Her neat white dress was crisp and fresh and her short hair gleamed in the sunlight. She was wearing light make-up as an indication that she had followed Laurel's advice to make her peace with her mother.

The chauffeur-driven Bertram-Smythe car dropped her there and went off again, leaving Barbie directing a curious glance at another car, sleek and black and powerful, that stood in the driveway.

Laurel came to the front door as she heard the car door slam and smiled a greeting at Barbie.

'You look a lot happier than you did yesterday.'

'I feel it.' She directed a slightly apprehensive glance at the other car. 'I didn't know you were having anyone else to lunch.'

'Well, I didn't intend to, but he insisted on coming too, so that he could set your mind at ease himself,' Laurel lied quite unblushingly.

'He!' Barbie's eyes widened in dismay. 'You mean Manoel?' She did not wait for any answer, but actually turned away, as if she was going to refuse to enter the house.

Laurel caught her arm. 'Wait a moment,' she said laughingly. 'You're not going to run away?'

Barbie shook her head, then nodded. 'I can't possibly see him,' she said frantically.

'Why not?' Manoel asked, appearing in the doorway himself.

'Oh!' Barbie went a vivid scarlet and just stood where she was. 'I ... I mean Mother. ...' She broke off, quite unable to go any further, then covered her confusion by turning indignantly to Laurel. 'I thought you said you'd explained everything.'

'I have, so you needn't start attacking me,' Laurel retorted equably. 'I suggest we go inside and discuss it sitting down. There's just time for a drink before dinner.'

In the cool little lounge she served Barbie and herself with chilled lemon squash and Manoel with something stronger. Barbie sipped her drink, still patently uneasy, darting surreptitious little glances at Manoel every now and again, while the other two carried on a light, friendly conversation to give her time to recover her aplomb.

Finally Barbie set her glass down on the table as if she had come to a decision.

'You ... you did understand, didn't you? That I ... I mean Mother ...'

Manoel's dark eyes twinkled. 'Yes?' he inquired politely.

Barbie shot him a scowling glance and appeared to recover quite considerably in what she no doubt deemed justified annoyance.

'You needn't be so obtuse. If Laurel explained, you know quite well what I'm talking about.' She stuck her small chin out pugnaciously. 'It's all Mother's idea. I wouldn't chase a man for anything.'

'*Pequeña*, you would not know how to if you tried,' Manoel laughed. 'You need have no worries. I know the situation well. Don't you think that I have parent troubles of my own?'

135

'Do you?' Barbie gave him a wondering glance. 'You mean that your parents do it too?' she asked unbelievingly.

He made a negligent gesture with one slender, brown hand. 'It seems to be the way of parents, only I do not have your courage. When it becomes too much, I jump on my yacht and run away. You manage to stay and face it.'

Barbie suddenly grinned, as if struck by the absurdity of someone as sophisticated and worldly-wise as Manoel certainly was, in spite of his slight air of reserve and shyness, being forced to flee from parental intrigue.

Then her gamin grin died. 'Still, it does make things so awkward sometimes,' she sighed. 'I know Mother means well, but I wish she wouldn't.'

Manoel murmured something in Portuguese and Laurel saw the younger girl's lips drawn down in a return of the impish grin usually so characteristic of her.

'Careful, Manoel,' she said laughingly, in case he made any unguarded remark. 'She understands Portuguese.' She rose to her feet, deeming it safe to leave them now that the first hurdle of Barbie's discomfort had been overcome. 'I'll go and see what's happened to our lunch and leave Barbie to try her accent out on you,' she added as she went out of the room, and heard Barbie say that she would not dare to as it was probably dreadful.

Round one to Manoel, she thought, as she entered the small, compact kitchen. Mr. Paul Brenton might think that he had secured Barbie's young heart, but he would find before long that he had very dangerous competition. Manoel might appear reserved and somewhat shy, but he doubtless had all the Latin's inherent knowledge of how to win a girl's love, added to which he was wise enough not to rush his fences.

Just try to beat that, Mr. Paul Brenton! she thought in great satisfaction. Experience was one thing, but genuine love was another, of far greater power.

CHAPTER SIX

LAUREL was arranging flowers in an earthenware vase when the telephone rang. She crossed the room and lifted the receiver. Instantly, when she recognized Stephen's voice, her fingers tightened involuntarily on the insensate black material of the receiver.

'Laurel speaking,' she said carefully, disturbed that her reaction should be so intense, when she had thought she had herself well under control.

'Good. Look, darling, I'm going down-coast this morning. Like to come?'

His voice was everything that a fiancé's should be and she wondered at it for a moment, until she remembered Ned mentioning that the telephonists often listened in. No doubt about it, when Stephen undertook anything, he made an excellent job of it, guarding against even gossiping telephone operators receiving the wrong impression. Partly for the same reason, but more because she was delighted at the prospect of being with him, she answered in the same tone.

'I'd love to!'

'Good. I'll pick you up in about fifteen minutes. We're going by boat. Better wear shorts. Can you be ready by then?'

'Easily.'

She rang off, stood there for a moment with one hand pressed to her mouth, telling herself again and again that it was just foolishness to feel so happy, when he had only invited her to go with him for the sake of appearances.

Nevertheless, she took particular pains with her appearance in the short time at her disposal, and at the very moment that his car drew up outside, she was standing on the step, looking young and attractive in tailored white shorts and a sleeveless blue blouse, the sun glinting

137

on the short curls that clustered all over her head.

Stephen himself was also wearing white shorts, and a short-sleeved white shirt that proved an effective foil for his tanned skin and black hair. He looked so attractive that she felt her heart give its usual little foolish skip that no amount of admonishment could ever control, but his grey eyes had an appraising look as they deliberately took in every detail of her own appearance.

'If you make any remarks about schoolteachers, I shall slap you,' she said, forestalling the remark she was certain he was on the point of making.

'You know what happens to little girls who do that,' he drawled, as he had once before.

'I've been finding out,' she retorted, 'without having to slap you.'

Stephen grinned and held open the car door. 'Console yourself, my child. At least you're still alive.'

Too much alive, she thought grimly. Too much alive and aware of him close at her side as he slid into the driving seat and started the engine.

'Where are we going?' she asked, deeming that a safe topic of conversation.

'I'm taking some medical supplies to a small planta-tion down coast. There is a road of sorts, but it's easier by sea.'

Laurel gave him a quick, curious glance. 'One of your own plantations?'

He quirked one infuriating eyebrow, without taking his eyes off the road.

'Inquiring into my financial status already?'

'No, I was not,' she snapped crossly. 'And I'm not even curious now.'

'Really?' He shot her a provocative side glance. 'I thought you might want to know for this breach of promise case you were talking about.'

Laurel held on to her temper with difficulty, telling herself that she had known quite well he would still annoy her, even if she did love him now. The only way out seemed to be to try to meet him on his own ground.

She nodded with a contemplative smile. 'Yes, I suppose a full statement of your financial status would be an essential exhibit,' she agreed academically, 'but I'm afraid your threat to make me marry you would be quite enough to deter me right from the start.'

He was silent for so long after that remark that she at last dared a quick glance at his face, to find him smiling faintly. He chose that moment to turn his head and catch her glance and the smile grew rueful.

'You pack quite a punch, don't you?'

'You asked for it,' she told him quickly.

He made no reply to that, but for a time concentrated on his driving as they were coming to the outskirts of Milton. Probably he personally considered he was entitled to make whatever remarks he chose without retaliation, she decided, and added to herself that she was not going to let him get away with it, whatever she felt about him. As she gazed about her, she was struck again by the Portuguese atmosphere of many of the buildings.

'I sometimes forget the island was originally Portuguese, until I see some of the older buildings,' she commented idly. 'How was it acquired by England?'

'By nothing so adventurous as fighting for it.' Again she felt that provocative glance on her. 'A little gold poured into Portuguese coffers acquired it as a base for trading ships. The new English governor of the island sealed the bargain by marrying old Dom Miguel's daughter.'

'And their son was Nicholas Barrington, Anthea's favourite ancestor,' Laurel said with a smile.

'So you've heard of him.'

'Very much so,' she laughed. 'Anthea would apparently like to be carried off by someone like him.'

'No doubt she would,' Anthea's brother agreed dryly. He shot her another of those aggravating side glances. 'What about you?'

Despite what she had said to Anthea, she had no intention whatsoever of admitting the same thing to Stephen. She had no doubt at all that it would lay her open to some jibing remark.

'He's very much like you, except that he has red hair,' she replied carefully, hoping that would be ambiguous enough.

'Meaning that you'd play safe.' He grinned as he swung the car into the kerb and drew up at the esplanade that fronted the harbour. 'I'm surprised you agreed to come this morning, knowing my ancestor's reputation.'

'I can swim quite well,' she countered demurely, and climbed out on to the footpath before he could come round to her side.

'Touché!' he acknowledged, and slammed the car door. 'Sure you didn't teach fencing at school, or is this the result of handling small boys?'

'Could be,' she retorted, and added daringly, 'perhaps there isn't much difference.'

Stephen shot her a quizzical look. 'I might ask you if you still think so later on,' he warned her as he took a wicker picnic basket and a large parcel from the back seat of the car.

'I might even give you an answer,' Laurel told him sweetly, and felt a rush of that reckless gaiety she had experienced on the first night of that mock engagement, the defiance she had known when Roberta's cold green eyes had met hers, glittering their message of icy dislike and the challenge to get back the man she had once possessed so completely.

She knew quite well what caused the feeling this time. The esplanade was fairly crowded and Stephen had been forced to leave his car some yards farther along from where his own yacht was moored – right opposite to a trim white hull emblazoned with the name *Firebird*.

That was the yacht which had brought Roberta to Ladrana, the yacht where perhaps, even now, she watched Stephen walk away towards his own craft – but he had not asked Roberta to go with him. She had that much out of this mock engagement. It would be she, Laurel Shannon, and not Roberta, who would go down-coast with him. She had a very human desire that Roberta would be watching, but almost instantly she decided that she wished otherwise, in case the beautiful, red-haired woman spoke to them and Stephen invited her to come as well. She could not help feeling that in that event she would be the unwanted third.

Moored alongside Stephen's yacht she saw the slender dart of a launch, more like a speed-boat than anything else, that had brought him into the harbour on her second day in Ladrana, the day she had been hating him so much and exasperated with Ned for blindly going off and leaving her with a man she had felt her brother should have recognized as being the type she would not have been left with from choice. A little whimsically she reflected on how much her ideas had changed since that day. Now her happiest choice would have been to be left with him for always.

There was only room for two in the powerful launch, which seemed to be all engine apart from the tiny seat space in front and a locker at the back.

Bending down, he picked up an oilskin that was lying on the seat and handed it to her.

'Better put this on. You're liable to get wet.'

While she drew it on, he opened the locker behind the seat and drew out a second oilskin, then placed the hamper and parcel securely in position, closed the snug-fitting door and drew on his own oilskin. The boat rocked slightly as she stepped down into it, then he had switched on the engine and it came to life with the coughing grunt of some primaeval monster awakened out of a deep sleep, then became muted to a deep, waiting throb. To her imagination it seemed to sing a song of restrained power, longing to get away from the confines of the harbour to the freedom of the sea.

They moved smoothly away from the quay and, as they

passed the moored *Rosaritos,* Manoel waved to them from the stern rail. They both waved back and Stephen called out something to him in Portuguese.

Laurel glanced at him curiously as he manoeuvred the craft out into clearer water. He caught her look and quirked that irritating eyebrow.

'What now?'

'I was just wondering how much Portuguese there is in you.'

'Enough.'

And just what was that supposed to mean? she thought exasperatedly. Enough for what? Enough to know that the blood could sing hotly in a man's veins, but not enough for it to become out of control?

They were clear of all the other craft now, the needle nose of the launch was pointed towards the headland and the open sea. Stephen's fingers were playing gently on the controls, the sound of the engine rising and falling, as if it was eager to be gone.

'Afraid of speed?'

She frowned dubiously. 'I don't think so.'

He opened up the throttle and the song of the engine mounted, the needle nose lifted from the water and the wake creamed frothily behind them. Higher the song of power mounted and with it the slender part of a ship thrust her nose arrogantly farther from the sea.

For a moment, as the launch had jumped forward under the surge of released power, she had felt the very faintest of qualms, but it was gone almost instantly and a heady thrill took its place.

'Faster!' she demanded impetuously.

Stephen glanced at her and grinned. Her oilskin was wet with spray and the short clustered curls were soaked, but her lips were parted in an eager smile and excitement danced in her eyes. His fingers closed almost caressingly on the throttle and opened it wide, so that the ship became a screaming devil of unleashed power, howling defiance at anything and anyone who chose to listen.

She flashed him a quick look as he took her hand and held it beneath one of his on the wheel and found him looking just as she had imagined he would when she had first heard this boat screaming into the harbour all those days ago, dark buccaneer face intent and assured, a tiny smile playing around his firm mouth, strong ruthless hands gripping the wheel – and her own hand – battling with a living demon of a ship that tried to get away from him and could not. In that moment, with the heady intoxication of sheer speed joining them, she felt nearer to him than ever before. It did not seem to matter that their engagement was only a farce, that its true reality would return when the demon song ended, for a little space of time he was hers in a way that Roberta could never share, because she could not imagine the sophisticated soignée Roberta Fransom being caught up in such thraldom. For this moment, so fleeting in the passing pageant of time, she could let herself believe that he was really hers.

They dropped the medical supplies at a wooden landing-stage, where a half-caste boy was to take them further inland to the plantation house, then swung round an outjutting promontory, along an almost straight stretch of coastline until they rounded another rock spur and came to a tiny bay, where the blue water murmured gently on a silver pale beach. Back of it was a flat, grassy stretch of land for about a hundred yards, gradually merging into wooded country. Arms of rock enclosed the little bay on both sides, almost as if they wanted to hide it, and on the side a ledge formed a natural stone quay.

Stephen snagged the rope around a narrow spur of rock and sprang out on to the ledge. From where he reached down a hand to help Laurel up, gripped hard on her wrist and almost lifted her to his side with effortless strength. Then he unfastened her oilskin and tossed it down into the boat, to be followed by his own.

'Well?' he swept a hand around him. 'Like it?'

'It's a lovely little place.'

She privately thought it one of the loveliest places she had ever seen, but her voice might have sounded stilted because she was trying to stop herself from being over-effusive. Any spot would have seemed beautiful when she was with Stephen.

He grinned at her teasingly, reading a different meaning into her cautious voice.

'What's the matter – frightened of being here alone with me?'

'Not in the least,' she retorted with a good attempt at airy unconcern.

She jumped lightly down from the rock on to the grass below and a soft thud behind her told her that he had done the same thing, but she would not turn round to him and pretended to be interestedly surveying the ground in front of her, even though she was acutely aware of him close behind her. When he put his arms around her from behind, as he had in Ned's garden, she was unable to stop herself stiffening.

'There's no need for pretence as we don't have an audience.'

Her voice sounded very prim and prudish, but at least that was better than being as tremulous as she felt inside – not that it seemed to have any effect on Stephen. If anything, his arms tightened, drawing her closer against him.

'I thought you said you weren't afraid.'

She turned her head to protest indignantly and instantly realized her mistake when his lips brushed hers in a mocking kiss that was as light as a butterfly's wing, then he released her, with no sign of the reluctance he would no doubt have shown had she been Roberta.

She busied herself with opening the picnic hamper he had dropped down on the grass, hoping that she looked as cool and unperturbed as he did, but wishing that he would not stand there regarding her so speculatively with those uncomfortably perceptive grey eyes.

To cover her too acute awareness of him, she handed

him a wrapped bundle.

'Here, make yourself useful, Stephen Barrington.'

'Yes, teacher.' He grinned as he dropped down at her side and took the package from her, unwrapped it to disclose a small chicken, which he neatly dismembered and set out on one of the plates the hamper contained, then covered the pieces with a white linen napkin until they were ready.

'Can I clean the blackboard now?' he asked.

She gave him a startled glance, then laughed. 'What makes you think that merits cleaning the blackboard?'

He pulled out one of her short curls and watched it spring back again.

'I thought teachers always allowed the good little boys to clean the blackboard.'

'I doubt very much whether you would have been one of the good little boys,' she retorted dryly.

'Perhaps not,' he agreed, and pulled out another of her short curls, seemingly intrigued by their elastic ability to wind themselves up again. 'This reminds me of spring wire,' he commented after a moment, pulling out a third one and letting go to watch it rewind itself tightly.

'Thank you, Stephen,' she retorted sweetly. 'I can think of nothing better than having my hair compared to wire.'

He grinned again. 'Don't fish for compliments. You know it's like silk.' He was threading both hands through it now, his fingers light and caressing. 'Smells fresh, like pine.'

'It's the shampoo I use.' She sat very still, willing her absurdly thrilling senses to order, then said very evenly, 'Are you trying to flirt with me, Stephen?'

'I never just try.' She refused to look at him, but nevertheless received an impression of mocking amusement. 'Do you mind?'

'Have a sandwich,' she countered, and perforce he had to drop one hand to take the plate she held out, but he laid the other arm negligently about her shoulders – at least it might be negligently to him. She felt the contact all through her.

'I asked you a question.'

'I thought you liked your women experienced,' she parried swiftly.

'That's a point – but even schoolteachers can learn.'

She debated whether she should object very strongly at that point. Quite obviously he was only amusing himself with her until he made up his mind about Roberta, but she could not decide just then whether she should whip up what pride remained and tell him to find someone else to fill in time with until he did make up his mind. She had no doubt that he would be able to do so and the question remained whether she should be weak enough to sink pride and just follow her stupid senses which yearned even for crumbs like this. In the end she decided to leave the matter to progress of its own accord for the moment.

She bit determinedly into a sandwich, as if to show that she was really more interested in lunch than philandering, finished it and leaned forward to reach into the basket for a piece of fruit, so that his arm fell away from her shoulders.

Stephen gave her a dryly quizzical glance. 'An adroit move, my child.' Up went that irritating eyebrow again, as he saw her expression. 'Are you about to object to being called a child again? How will *querida* do instead?'

'What does it mean?' she asked cautiously.

'Maybe I'll tell you some day.'

'It's Portuguese, isn't it?' When he nodded, she added, 'Then maybe I'll ask Manoel.'

For a brief moment the very faintest suspicion of a frown came over his face, then he grinned with his usual exasperating amusement that seemed to suggest lazy toleration of her youth and inexperience.

'Better wait until you know him a little better.'

Laurel smiled, but made no answer to that. Privately she considered she knew him quite well enough by now to ask the meaning of one simple word, whatever it might be, after all the conspiring she had gone about Barbie.

Stephen watched her with the lazy amusement still playing around his firm mouth and dancing in the grey eyes.

'Perhaps I might ask you what that smile means.'

'Perhaps you might, but I doubt whether you would get an answer,' she retorted, a spark of independence squaring her small, determined chin. Really, did Stephen think that a make-believe engagement even gave him the right to inquire into her most private thoughts?

'All right. Don't go all prickly,' he said calmly, in such a manner that she felt as if she had been indulging in a childish tantrum.

'Oh, you . . .!' She broke off, biting her lips, and reached crossly for a piece of chicken to add to her varied diet, only to find that it contained the wishbone, a circumstance which she considered most incongruous. She knew what she wished for, but she knew equally well that it could never come true, so she went to toss it away after she had eaten the tender white meat.

Stephen's hand caught her wrist. 'Aren't you going to wish?'

She shrugged. 'I know it won't come true, so why bother?'

'Defeated from the start!' He picked up the piece of bone and held it out to her. 'Come on, you little coward, take a chance.'

Love him? She eyed him with positive dislike. 'Stop calling me a coward!'

'Well, aren't you?' he asked derisively. 'Afraid of life, afraid of falling in love. Even afraid to wish in case it comes true.'

'Certainly not!' She flushed indignantly. 'I merely know that what I want to wish for is impossible and I refuse to wish for something that's only second best.' With a defiant movement she caught hold of a forked branch of the wishbone and jerked violently, to find herself left with the smaller piece, which she was quite certain only confirmed that her wish was useless. 'Well, does that satisfy you?' she demanded.

Stephen grinned. 'You don't need to worry. I have the part that counts.'

And it would be so easy for his wish to come true. She had no doubt at all what he would have wished for. All he had to do was restrain his impatience for a little while, until this mock engagement could be played out, then he could just reach out a hand and take what he really wanted.

She watched him scoop out a little hole in the sand and carefully bury the piece of broken wishbone, and it sent the stabbing pain of longing through her heart again, because the simple, almost childish action told her once again how very human the assured, worldly and exasperating Stephen Barrington really was under his sophistication.

She forced a smile she hoped was natural. 'You're burying that as if your wish means a lot to you.'

He looked up and momentarily his dark face was more serious than she had ever seen it before.

'I've just realized how much it does mean to me,' he said quietly.

Again pain stabbed through her heart, because she knew that he must have realized, perhaps at the very moment that her fingers snapped the wishbone, how much Roberta meant to him and how little her previous defect counted.

'I hope it comes true, then,' she replied generously, and tried to believe that the stab of pain would not always be there when she thought of Roberta in his arms.

A tantalizing smile curved his lips and there was something puzzling in his eyes, a challenging amusement she could find no reason for.

'Thank you, *querida*. If it comes true, I'll tell you what it was.'

'Good. I'll keep you to it.' She spoke briskly, to stifle a

mad urge to cry out wildly that Roberta would never make him happy, that he deserved somebody who could give him a finer and far less selfish love, even if it was not herself.

After they had emptied the flask of coffee, Stephen decided they had better start on the return journey and Laurel watched the little bay dropping behind her, knowing she would always remember it, because here she had known happiness and pain, here she had had Stephen to herself for a short space of time – and here also he had finally come to the conclusion that he must have Roberta, whatever she was like under her beauty.

As they moved out, through the outjutting arms of rock, she looked back at the pale crescent of beach that sloped upwards to grass and woodlands. There was a wistful little smile on her lips as she decided that she would never go back there, whoever offered to take her, because it was unlikely that she would ever go there again with Stephen.

They swung round the spur of rock and the little bay was lost from sight; the engine opened up with a powerful roar and they were skimming along the straight stretch of coastline, round the promontory to see the wooden landing stage in the distance, where they had dropped the medical supplies, and the sight of it seemed somehow to make the journey already at an end, even though they still had a long way to go.

When they did at last come in sight of the harbour, she was almost glad of it – though not so glad when Roberta appeared at the stern rail of *Firebird*.

'Come and join me for coffee,' she called out. 'I've just had some made. The others have gone in to town. I was hoping somebody would come along, so I wouldn't have to drink it alone.'

Stephen glanced round at the girl at his side before answering. 'Want to go up, or are you in a hurry to return home?'

Laurel's first inclination was to say she would not step

on board the yacht that had brought Roberta to the island, not if she could possibly help it, then she realized that not only would it sound outrageously rude, but that Stephen probably wished to go.

'I'm not in any hurry,' she said instead, and steeled herself to meet the hidden dislike and warning she knew would be in Roberta's beautiful green eyes.

When they climbed aboard, Roberta immediately contrived to make her feel a total wreck. Laurel knew that her white shorts, which had been so fresh and clean when she started out in the morning, were crumpled now and even grubby in places, where she had sat on the sand and grass, and her blouse was stained at the neck with sea-water where she had not fastened the oilskin properly. Luckily nothing could affect the natural curl in her hair, so it did not hang down limp and bedraggled after its soaking in sea-water, but she was well aware that it was stiff with salt and wild with the effect of the wind. Roberta on the other hand looked trim and crisp in spotless white slacks and a cool, green blouse, her wonderful red hair coiled smoothly about her finely shaped head.

She held out both hands to Stephen with a smile that showed perfect and gleaming teeth. To Laurel's eyes Stephen seemed to take them with perfect composure, but she wondered if Roberta's touch affected him as much as his did when he made her the recipient of one of his light, mocking caresses. She wanted to believe that he took her hands so unhesitatingly because it would have been rude to ignore them, but she knew quite well it was not so even though he did disengage himself almost immediately.

'I watched you go by this morning,' Roberta said. 'I hoped you would have a good day.'

Was that a gentle reproach to Stephen for not having invited her?

'It looks as if you did enjoy yourself,' she added, which remark immediately made Laurel feel like a grubby schoolchild who had come home with sticky paws and clothes rather the worse for wear.

'We did,' Stephen replied equably. He slanted a glance at Laurel. 'Didn't we, darling?'

'Lovely,' she agreed.

Roberta led the way into a well-appointed lounge that Laurel decided she did not like half so much as the one she had been in on Manoel's yacht. It was tastefully furnished, but she told herself that she did not like all the modernistic chromium fittings, even while she knew quite well the real reason for her dislike.

As Roberta had said, coffee was already waiting upon the table, either from lucky chance or she had sighted them the moment they entered the harbour and instantly ordered coffee made. She seemed quite at home issuing orders on the yacht, even though it did not belong to her. A steward brought in two more cups at her instructions and Roberta poured out the fragrant, steaming liquid and handed their cups across the table to them.

Laurel sipped hers slowly, and even though Roberta appeared to be making them welcome, she wished she was on the *Rosaritos* with Stephen sitting opposite her instead of Manoel, much as she liked the young Portuguese, or on Stephen's own yacht – anywhere where Roberta would not be present.

Roberta smiled across at her with every appearance of friendliness. 'How are you finding Stephen as a fiancé, Miss Shannon?' She laughed and made a deprecating movement with one hand. 'Or shouldn't I ask such a personal question?'

Laurel met her glance coolly. 'Not at all. I think he makes a wonderful fiancé.'

Stephen grinned. 'Thank you, darling. Loyal to the end.'

'Of course he likes his own way,' his fiancée added.

Roberta nodded. 'He always did,' she murmured. 'He hasn't changed a bit. Take a word of advice, Miss Shannon. Don't let him get away with it too often, or there'll be no controlling him at all.'

'I have no intention of letting him get away with it,' Laurel replied, hoping her voice sounded as careless and amused as she tried to make it appear.

She wondered what Stephen thought of this verbal sparring between them. He probably knew that Roberta still loved him and was astute enough to recognize her remarks for what they were, since she obviously did not know the truth. That was the one thing that puzzled her. She felt sure that he would have explained to Roberta, at least, what had happened, and probably he would, now that he had finally made up his mind.

Roberta turned her smiling glance on Stephen. 'On second thoughts, I think you must have changed, Stephen, to let your fiancée go to visit an attractive man alone on his yacht.'

Laurel watched Stephen turn his grey glance on her and raise an interrogatory brow.

'You have me curious. Who is this attractive man you've been meeting in secret, my child?'

'Oh dear, I hope I haven't given anything away that I shouldn't,' Roberta said apologetically. 'I took it for granted that you knew.'

'Liar,' Laurel said to herself. 'I think Mrs. Fransom means Manoel,' she said aloud, as casually as she could manage, because she was seething inside. Roberta, she was quite sure, had invited them aboard simply and solely to impart that little item of information to Stephen, and had it been a normal engagement she might have done a great deal of harm. As it was, she must be quite disappointed in Stephen's reaction. He looked supremely unconcerned.

'So you've been meeting Manoel on the quiet, have you?' he drawled affectionately. 'Remind me to beat you when we get home.'

Roberta laughed and allowed the conversation to drift along on to another topic. If she did feel any disappointment at the reception her remark had received she did not show any sign of it.

The subject was not touched on again in Roberta's presence and, from his reception of the remark at the time it had been made, Laurel thought that Stephen had been so uninterested in the fact that she had gone to see Manoel that he had forgotten all about it. Consequently she was surprised when he brought it up in the car, as he was driving her back home.

He tossed his slim gold cigarette case into her lap, as he had once before.

'Light me a cigarette, will you?'

Silently she did so and handed it to him. He slid the cigarette case into his pocket again, then shot her a glance of rather unkind mockery.

'So you're providing me with a rival already?'

Laurel gave him a startled glance. 'What do you mean?'

'The attractive man you were meeting on his yacht.'

'Manoel?'

He nodded and his glance, as mocking and derisive as when she had first known him, went over her again.

'I think Roberta's right. I should object. Manoel is far too attractive for you to be visiting him alone.'

'Don't be ridiculous!' Laurel snapped. 'Anyway, you would have no right to object, even if I did go to visit him.'

'Then you did go to see him?'

'Yes, I did.'

'Mind telling me why?'

'It was . . .' she broke off, realizing she could not tell him something that concerned only Barbie and Manoel. 'It was a personal matter,' she finished instead.

'So it seems,' he agreed. 'Very personal.' Again that grey glance slid over her, full of satirical mockery. 'I take back everything I said about you being a coward. Just remember that with Manoel you're playing with fire. He might be reserved, but he's all Portuguese.'

Laurel flushed uncomfortably. 'Don't be so ridiculous,' she said again. 'It . . . it's nothing of the kind. . . .'

'Methinks the lady doth protest too much.' He swung

the car adroitly round a sharp corner and added, 'Don't panic. Even schoolteachers have to learn about falling in love.' There was another pause, while he negotiated a second tricky bend and came on to a straight stretch of road. 'I begin to understand now why you were so unresponsive this morning.'

'Perhaps I'm old-fashioned enough to want to go to the man I eventually marry without a whole string of affairs behind me,' she was stung into retorting.

Stephen's hands tightened on the wheel. 'I don't know whether I should kiss you or spank you for that last remark,' he said thinly.

'Well, if you can't make up your mind – I would prefer to be kissed,' she flashed back.

'That's quite an admission.'

'Is it?' Her breath was coming fast now and she regarded him with defiant eyes. 'A kiss is soon over. A spanking often leaves after-effects which are also unpleasant.'

She heard him mutter something under his breath at that and she was aghast at what she had said, wondering how they had so suddenly lost the rather dangerous friendship that had been between them. Now they were acting almost as if they were deadly enemies.

After that he hardly spoke to her for the rest of the journey and she was angry and miserable at the same time, bitter with Roberta that she should have so deliberately brought up the subject and furious with Stephen for his quite unwarranted follow-up of it. After all, what business was it of his who she went to visit when he cared nothing at all for her?

At the door of Ned's house he braked the car sharply and flicked the emerald ring on her hand with a derogatory finger.

'We'll get rid of that bauble as soon as possible, now that your attention is definitely engaged elsewhere.'

Laurel immediately wrenched at the ring and pulled it off. 'You can have it back right now!' she retorted.

He took the ring from her and pushed it back into place with ungentle fingers. 'Leave it there for the time being. It's too soon yet.' He looked down at her with eyes that were almost cruel. 'I can appreciate your anxiety to be free. Don't worry. We won't keep up this farce any longer than necessary. I imagine that's what you want.'

'You're quite right. That is just what I do want,' and before she could break down into humiliating tears, she jumped out of the car and ran into the house, but there, out of sight of the man she had left so tempestuously, she allowed the tears to run unchecked down her face. She heard the sound of the car drawing away as she ran up the stairs to her room, mercifully meeting neither Ned nor Pepita on the way, and looked down at the empty driveway from her window.

All anger was gone now. All that was left was a cold emptiness and the knowledge that, whatever else Roberta had set out to do, she had certainly destroyed the thin, tenuous thread of friendship that had joined her to Stephen. No, that was not all that was left – not quite. She was burdened also with a love that she knew to be quite hopeless and, it seemed, enduring.

What had she once called it – a dead-end avenue with heartbreak at the end of it? Well, the heartbreak had certainly started.

CHAPTER SEVEN

LAUREL was not in the least surprised when Anthea breezed in the following morning and exhibited every intention of settling down to one of those heart-to-heart chats the elder girl had almost come to dread, since it seemed that, however much she might make up her mind at the beginning, somehow they still resulted in the wily and adroit Miss Barrington managing to manoeuvre her into a position which was not only quite against her will, but also afforded her considerable surprise later on at finding that she had allowed herself to be so expertly manoeuvred, when she had known all along that she was being subjected to subtle and expert tactics to that very end.

However, this particular morning, Laurel considered that she seemed to be escaping fairly lightly, unless of course her careful answers in response to Anthea's gay, chattering questions gave away more than she realized, which was not at all beyond the bounds of possibility. She made no mention of Stephen's attempt to make love to her on the island, nor did she mention their quarrel after Roberta's delicate and highly successful interference; but some sign of the latter disturbance must still have been evident when Stephen reached Castelanto, since Anthea broke off quite suddenly in the middle of gay chatter about nothing in particular.

'Just what did you say to Stephen to send him home in such a black temper?' she asked with a frown, quite as if she had all the right in the world to know all the intimate details that would have to come to light to fully answer such a question, an attitude which was quite plain to Laurel who, because she was still feeling upset and miserable over the way in which she had parted from Stephen the day before, was not surprised to detect a touch of asperity in her reply.

'I don't think that's any business of yours, Anthea. Having succeeded in placing both of us in such an unbearable position, you shouldn't be surprised when it occasionally leads us to quarrel.'

Anthea whistled softly. 'It must have been quite a row,' she commented, without the least sign of apology for bringing up a subject which quite obviously was extremely delicate and still disturbed the girl beside her.

'Why not ask Stephen himself?' Laurel retorted.

'I might at that,' agreed the provocative Miss Barrington.

Quite suddenly Laurel felt that it was all becoming

too much for her. They were quite heartless, these Barringtons! Anthea determined to twist circumstances to fit her own plans and Stephen playing lightly at love while he made up his mind whether it was worth accepting Roberta, with his eyes open this time.

'Anthea, I don't want to ask you to go, but if you say one more word on the subject, I shall. It must be quite obvious to you that Stephen is in love with Roberta.'

Instantly contrite, Anthea caught her arm as Laurel turned away to hide the involuntary tears that started to her eyes.

'Laurel, I'm sorry,' she said softly, with what, for her, was almost diffidence.

Laurel bit her lips to stop their trembling, before she turned back to shrug with assumed indifference.

'Let's drop the subject, shall we?' She picked up a few sheets of paper that had been dropped on the table at Anthea's arrival. 'I've been drafting out a few notes for Mrs. B-S.'

After this, probably because even the Barringtons could not be completely heartless, Anthea took up her cue and did not pursue the previous subject.

'About the Greek dancing, you mean?'

Laurel nodded, glad to find that the previous subject was abandoned – for the moment.

'Are you interested?' Before Anthea could reply she added quickly, 'I warn you, it's quite strenuous. It would take up a fair amount of your time.'

'I have plenty of spare time.'

With the knowledge that Anthea had probably never done a day's work in her life and Castelanto, run by an extremely efficient housekeeper, had no need of her attention, Laurel did not pursue that particular subject.

She went on briskly, trying to keep her mind off Stephen, 'Have a glance at these notes. You'll see what I've mapped out and the type of people we shall need. You might know of others who would be interested.'

Anthea shot her a quick glance, but she took the notes

without comment, read them through and then nodded.

'They're clear enough. The men will be the problem, of course. The poor dears usually have a thing about being seen on the stage.' A faint return of the usual impish smile crossed the perfect features. 'I think I could persuade them, though.'

'I don't doubt that you could,' Laurel retorted somewhat dryly. The Barrington methods of persuasion rarely failed, whatever it was they embarked upon.

Anthea was riffling through the sheets of paper, gnawing at her underlip thoughtfully. 'You'll want somebody quite striking for the part of the king of the underworld in the final scene,' she commented, referring to the short ballet which concluded the programme, set around the old legend of the abduction of Persephone by Hades, king of the underworld. She hesitated a moment, then added, with a hint of the unusual diffidence she had displayed earlier, 'Do you think Stephen would . . . ?'

'I don't doubt that Stephen would look very appropriate for the part,' Laurel interrupted, 'but I doubt whether he would agree to do it. In any event,' she added, in case Anthea offered to use her powers of persuasion on her brother, 'I would prefer not to have him in it.'

'All right,' Anthea agreed. 'I think I could get Peter Marshall, if he would do.'

'Peter Marshall?' Laurel wrinkled up her brows thoughtfully, then nodded. 'Oh yes, I remember him.' An afternoon to remember also, the day when she had first had to hide from Stephen's too perceptive eyes the unwelcome fact that this sister had matchmaking plans for them, even to the extent of carrying Peter Marshall off into the garden to leave a clear field for Stephen himself.

Oh yes, she remembered Peter Marshall all right, because he had figured in one of those momentous meetings with Stephen – which never seemed to be like meetings with any other man – quite apart from the fact that she was in love with him. With the prospect of spending an afternoon or evening with Stephen in mind, one always knew that it would begin differently from a meeting with anyone else and most certainly end in an equally unpredictable manner. She was not quite sure whether that was part of the Barrington charm, or a reason to dislike them, but that did not of course stop anyone losing a heart or two to them, knowing it was quite hopeless but being in the unfortunate position of not being able to do a thing about it.

She realized after a moment that Anthea was watching her closely, with that too sharp Barrington perception, and she hastily brought her thoughts into order.

'Let me know as soon as you can whether he'll do it, then.'

Anthea nodded. 'Are you going to take part in it yourself?'

'No, not if I can help it. I shall have enough to do putting the thing together.' Another half-formed thought at the back of her mind was that it was not fair to the others for her to participate, with the knowledge of the years it had taken to bring the easy, liquid flow to her body with some of the dance movements demanded. There would be too sharp a comparison for the audience to make.

'I have complete sets of all the music we used in England,' she went on, and was relieved to find that by this time Anthea's interest was so genuinely caught she had completely abandoned all thought of holding an inquest on what had happened between Stephen and his supposed fiancée.

'What about Barbie?' Anthea asked after a time.

'She says she doesn't want to do any dancing, but I think it's just shyness. I can probably persuade her, although I don't want to do it against her will.'

Anthea shot her a suddenly sharp glance, proof that her agile mind was not completely absorbed in the dance programme.

'That Brenton man is still on the island.' She grimaced. 'I wish we could blackmail him into leaving somehow.'

Laurel did not comment on the absurdity of such criminal tendencies. Instead she shrugged, knowing that matter at least was well in hand.

'I expect he'll lose interest and look for fresh fields to conquer before long.'

Anthea shook her head. 'Not until he's done some damage,' she said grimly. 'I know his type – and Barbie's too nice to be in his clutches. I don't know how she stands the man.'

'He does have a kind of facile charm, I suppose,' Laurel conceded, 'and Barbie is too inexperienced to be able to see through him.'

Anthea made a sound that was remarkably like a grunt. 'You're inexperienced enough, but you can see through him. I wish Manoel would get a move on.' She grinned suddenly. 'For a Portuguese, he's awfully slow.'

'He's probably making sure he doesn't rush his fences,' Laurel said carefully. She had no particular wish to discuss Barbie's private affairs – especially after the way Manoel had become involved in her quarrel with Stephen – but at least it did keep Anthea's mind off the quarrel, until the conversation could be turned into impersonal channels again.

'He'd better not wait too long, or he'll find there's no bird on the fence to catch,' Anthea retorted, somewhat originally if ambiguously, Laurel thought.

'I think we can safely leave that to Manoel.'

Anthea nodded thoughtfully. 'There's a lot more to Manoel than meets the eye. He probably knows just what's going on and how to handle it,' which was quite an admission for her and one with which, remembering her own conversation with Manoel, Laurel fully agreed.

Manoel would no doubt catch his wild bird in the end, Stephen would marry Roberta and Anthea would some day or the other choose one of the men who flocked around her – while the foolish Shannons would just have to go on eating their hearts out for something they could not have.

160

With Anthea's departure, Laurel settled down to prepare an English lunch, leaving Pepita engaged in the semi-spring-clean of the house she embarked upon every week-end, in addition to the daily cleaning, much to the amusement of both Shannons. The little house positively sparkled and she would indignantly refuse any help from the owner's newly arrived sister, under the impression apparently that young, pretty girls should spend all their time enjoying themselves. Laurel had let her have her own way with the house, but put her foot down in the kitchen.

Ned, hot and dusty from a morning in the fields, popped his head around the kitchen door and grinned, with an appreciative sniff at the savoury aroma coming from the direction of the stove.

'Smells good. What is it?'

Laurel smiled. 'It doesn't have a name. Just something of my own concoction. You can name it after you've tasted it.'

'Right.' He disappeared outside with another grin, leaving Laurel to her thoughts again, which thoughts seemed to have a bad habit of catching up with her whatever she was doing.

Anthea, of course, was quite capable of asking Stephen outright what the quarrel had been about, but it was extremely doubtful that Stephen would give her a satisfactory reply. She found that she had to revise her estimate of him somewhat and admit that he was not in the least conceited about his personal attraction, but he would no doubt still find that it rankled a little that the girl he was supposed to be engaged to, in the eyes of the world at least, found him of so little interest that she was already allowing her name to be coupled with someone else. In one way, though, she could not help being rather glad he had received the impression that she was in love with Manoel and that he returned her supposed affection. The young Portuguese was attractive and quite as eligible as Stephen himself. It was also an additional safeguard against Stephen learning the full extent of her change of heart about him. If he thought she was in love with somebody else, he would not be so quick to pick up any slip she might make as to the true state of affairs.

Ned came back into the kitchen, his hair still wet from his bath and his sun-tanned skin glowing with health. His own hopeless love for the other member of the Barrington household did not seem to be affecting him as much as it did her, his sister decided, although of course appearances were very deceptive. She was continually surprised when she looked into her mirror and saw the reflection of her own glowing youth, apparently burdened with no cares, when she was certain she should look quite haggard after a sleepless night spent trying to reason out just why she should have fallen in love with someone so eminently unsuitable. Ned probably felt just as hurt inside as she did. In fact she was sure of it sometimes when she caught a weary, dispirited look on his face, or a painfully wry smile in his eyes when he looked at Anthea. His eyes at the moment, though, were unusually perceptive. They even in a way reminded her uncomfortably of Stephen.

'Something wrong, pet?' he asked quietly after a moment.

Laurel shrugged, stirring the fragrant brew on the stove. 'What should be wrong?' She attempted a smile which she hoped was quite gay. 'It's a beautiful day and I have my favourite brother home to lunch.'

Ned grinned, but he quickly became serious again. 'Quarrelled with Steve?'

On the point of denying it, Laurel changed her mind. Ned in this mood could be obstinate.

'Not exactly,' she said carefully.

'Anything serious?' He picked up her hand and twisted the emerald ring with something like relief. 'At least you're still engaged to him.' He gave her a sharp glance. 'Better watch out for that Fransom woman, pet. She'll cause trouble if she can. She's out to get him back.'

'She will get him back.'

The words were out before she could stop them, coming so naturally, because it was what she believed herself.

Ned shook his head. 'No man would take back a woman who had treated him the way Roberta Fransom did Stephen.' He grinned, but his expression was still faintly worried. 'Brace up, pet. Stephen's no fool.' Again he threw her that sharp, perceptive glance. 'Did you quarrel over her?'

'No . . . well, not exactly.'

Suddenly, with no warning, with no intention of doing so, she found herself pouring out the whole story and Anthea's incredible part in what had happened, watching her brother's face grow blank with astonishment.

Ned whistled softly when she finished. 'No wonder you look down in the dumps!' He turned her to face him gently. 'There's one thing that Anthea didn't make up, though, isn't there?' As she remained silent, he added softly, 'You really are in love with him.'

She nodded wordlessly. There seemed no point in denying it. In a way it even helped, because Ned was undergoing exactly the same thing.

He laughed wryly and released her. 'We certainly are a pair of prize idiots.' He saw a suspicious brilliance in her eyes and immediately slipped his arm round her again. 'Want to have a cry?'

'No, thanks, Ned.' She freed herself and turned back to the stove, flicking away a surreptitious tear. 'Can't afford it at the moment. The lunch might burn,' she added in an attempt to bring the conversation back to normal. Mentally though she echoed his words. If ever a pair of prize idiots were born, it was the Shannon brother and sister, to fall in love with Anthea and Stephen Barrington.

With the perversity of fate in such matters, the next time Laurel saw Stephen she was actually in the company of Manoel and, because the situation between the young Portuguese and herself was so well defined and uncomplicated, her attitude was far less strained than it had ever been with Stephen, a fact which was apparently not lost on him as he came up to them, standing together on the quay, with the trim shape of *Rosaritos* behind them.

One black brow jerked up in the irritating way that was supremely his own and, in spite of the longing in her heart, she felt an uprush of the familiar annoyance.

'Good morning, Stephen,' she said quickly, before he could get in first with any telling remark which would send the colour to her face and perhaps give cause for Manoel to look rather puzzled. It was all very well to allow Stephen to believe that the attractive young Portuguese was in love with her, but an altogether different matter to have her bluff called in front of Manoel himself.

'Good morning, *pequeña*,' Stephen replied, but there was still a rather devilish lift to that dark brow which told her there was more to come. 'I'm sorry I can't greet you more warmly, but I don't think it would be appreciated at the moment.'

'Much too public,' she agreed, deliberately misunderstanding him, although both knew quite well that he referred to Manoel not appreciating the sight of another man kissing the girl he was in love with.

Manoel chose that moment to smile in amused understanding, which she was quite sure only strengthened the altogether wrong impression in Stephen's mind.

'Will you join me for a drink?' The attractive smile flashed across his dark face again. 'I was about to invite Laurel aboard until I remembered that her fiancé probably has enough Portuguese in him to regard it as rather incorrect.'

Manoel's words were plainly joking, to Laurel at least, knowing him as she did now, she was quite certain he would have never said a word out of place to her, even had he been in love with her, while she was still bound by the outward appearance of her engagement to Stephen, but the other man of course again entirely misinterpreted the remark. There was no mistaking the narrowing of the grey eyes and the derisive lift to the thin, almost cruel mouth.

'Most incorrect,' he drawled, and those too sharp eyes flicked to his fiancée's desperately controlled smile, which felt as if it had become fixed there. 'Just lately I've been wondering whether I might be more of a throwback to old Dom Miguel than I'd realized before.'

Again Manoel smiled and again he only plunged them further into the morass of misunderstanding.

'I do not think that Laurel will have cause to complain. She will at least agree that those with Portuguese blood know how to make love to a girl.'

Laurel saw the smiling amusement in his eyes and knew that he was once again only teasing her, with the usual Latin lack of embarrassment when speaking about love, looking directly at her and putting an altogether different construction on the flags of embarrassment that warmed her face.

'Well, my sweet, do you agree?' he drawled.

Laurel tilted her head defiantly. 'Of course.' She forced a smile she hoped was good enough to deceive. 'It's more than I dare do to disagree.'

'You show wisdom,' Manoel laughed. 'And now, will you join me for that drink?'

'Well, shall we, darling?'

With Stephen's almost cruel grip on her elbow already turning her towards the yacht, Laurel found she had no choice but to agree, so once again she tilted her head with that defiantly gay smile.

'I'd love to, Manoel.'

They mounted the gangway to the well scrubbed decks she remembered so well from her last visit. This time there seemed to be more of the crew around and a loud, excited burst of Portuguese came from the forward end of the vessel, to be quelled in one short sentence from Manoel. Almost as he spoke, he turned to them with the teasing smile once again evident.

'You must get Stephen to teach you Portuguese, Laurel.

He will no doubt find it useful on occasion.'

'I should imagine it would be quite a good language for making love in,' Laurel agreed, deciding that to take the war into the enemy camp was the only way to keep her head above water, with which bunch of mixed metaphors running through her mind she glanced unobtrusively at Stephen to see how he had taken it. By his expression she guessed she had only just forestalled the same sort of remark coming from him.

His eyes glinted with a strange, grey fire. 'An excellent language for the purpose,' he agreed, with almost a snap in his voice. 'But I rather think that Laurel has someone else in mind as an instructor.'

'But what better way than to learn it from the man one loves?' Manoel asked her teasingly.

The question was quite obviously directed at her, but it was Stephen who replied, tersely and to the point.

'Precisely.' He swung suddenly towards the rail. 'I'll have to miss that drink after all. Something slipped my memory. I think I'd better get back to Castelanto straight away.' The mocking grey glance slid over to Laurel, held her own shrinking one for a moment, then went on to Manoel. 'I don't think the conventions would be outraged if Laurel stayed for a drink.'

Without another word, before they could even make an attempt to stop him, while the look of surprise was still on Manoel's face, he swung quickly and lightly down to the quay and they watched his tall, arrogant figure striding along the stone flags to where the powerful maroon car was parked at the far end.

There was a puzzled silence for a long moment. Even the vociferous crew members had chosen that particular moment to cease every scrap of conversation. Hardly a breeze played over the sea. The yacht was still, the sails close furled and mute.

'*Pequeña*, you have quarrelled with Stephen?' Manoel asked at last, very quietly.

Laurel nodded. A quarrel was as simple an explanation as anything and he would understand what he thought was a lovers' quarrel.

She felt a gentle touch on her shoulder and turned to find him smiling sympathetically.

'It will pass, little one. Do not worry.' The smile grew a little teasing again. 'These quarrels make the reconciliation all the sweeter.'

For her and Stephen though there would be no reconciliation. She bit her lips deliberately, to still their trembling, and nodded with a brave acceptance she was far from feeling.

'I suppose so. But they hurt at the time.'

Manoel smiled again and turned her towards a gaily painted deck lounge.

'I will get you that drink, because I think you need it, then I will take you home, because I do not think Stephen would like you to stay here long in his present mood,' he added, with the teasing inflection back in his voice.

She felt like saying that Stephen would not care how long she remained on *Rosaritos*, but bit back the retort and nodded gratefully as he turned to go into the cabin.

Had ever a holiday been more blighted? She had come out to Ladrana with such high expectations in her heart. True, she had not meant to stay here permanently, because her independent nature would not allow her to live off Ned without giving anything in return. Then for a time she had believed that she could stay on the island, that Mrs. Dalkeith's idea of a kindergarten and vacation school would work, but she knew differently now. It would be impossible to stay on Ladrana after her engagement to Stephen was broken off, as very soon it must be. She could not endure much more of the strain those last two encounters with him had caused her, nor could she remain and watch him marry Roberta.

No, the safest and best thing was to go back to England, to put all thought of this beautiful island and the man it would always remind her of, far from her mind, even though she knew that she was going to find that so hard as to be almost impossible. But hard work would help. She would go back to teaching and try to forget that a deliberately provoking voice had once drawled, 'Even teachers must learn,' and every time she involuntarily remembered what he had taught her, the bittersweet inevitability of falling in love, she would throw herself just a little harder into her work and not think about a man with grey eyes and an aquiline, tanned face, she would not remember a voice that could be caressing as well as mocking, nor lean brown hands that could render her helpless with a touch – and above all she would not think of lips that had proved quite ridiculously false her professed dislike of him and turned it into love.

Laurel looked up with a smile she hoped was not as false as it felt when Manoel reappeared from the cabin. He handed one glass to her and then stood at the side of the lounge, holding the second glass in a thin, sensitive hand, looking down at her with a rather shrewd light in his dark eyes.

'Is it Roberta Fransom?' he asked quietly after a moment.

She gave him a swift, upward glance, then looked as quickly away.

'No . . . not entirely.'

He smiled and shook his head. 'Do not let her worry you, *pequeña*. A woman who has once revealed herself as she did. . . .' He broke off and shrugged. 'She can have no more influence.'

Much he knew, she thought, with a bitter little twist to her lips.

'You do not wish to talk about it? Then come, I will drive you home.'

He held out his hand to assist her to her feet, took the empty glass and placed it by the side of his own on a small, painted table by the side of the lounge, not in the least offended by her reluctance to discuss the matter, but conveying a quiet sympathy and understanding that was more welcome than any words could have been.

When they reached the quay Stephen's car had long since disappeared, but Roberta was idly smoking in the bows of the *Firebird* with the other members of the yacht party. Her keen eyes no doubt took in every gesture of the couple who had just left *Rosaritos*, which would in due course be reported cleverly and subtly to Stephen, Laurel decided, with a quick uprush of the bitterness she was beginning to know so well where Roberta was concerned.

Roberta waved to them languidly as they passed, but none of the party made any effort to detain them as they went along to where another of those dark, powerful monsters was parked, hired by Manoel for the duration of his stay on the island.

By tacit consent neither of them said a word until the car was moving and the quay – and Roberta – behind them and out of sight. Then Manoel gave a grim little nod.

'I find my dislike for that one increasing with the passing of each day.'

Laurel gave him a rueful little smile. 'I agree with you entirely.'

'Do not worry, little one. Soon she will be gone, and . . .'

'And there will be peace again?' she finished as he paused. 'I hope so,' she added, in a little bitter jest at fate. It would be Laurel Shannon, though, who would be leaving the island, not Roberta. She would stay in triumphant possession of the man she had meant to win back from the moment she set her dainty and expensively shod foot on the island.

'But of course there will be peace again – and happiness,' Manoel said softly. 'How else could it be?'

'Yes, how else could it be?' she echoed, but she was careful to turn her head away, so that he could not see the expression on her face. Much as she liked him, she had no wish to confide in Manoel. It was more than her pride could stand and, since that was just about all she had left, she felt she was justified in pandering to it. Ned and

Anthea knowing was quite enough.

For some time they drove in silence, the town behind them now, the road rising steeply to the flower-surrounded bungalows that were splashes of colour as they passed, then when they were almost at the ridiculously belligerent little cottage Ned and she occupied, Manoel reduced speed suddenly and backed the car. It was not until then, so deep had she been in her own thoughts, that she noticed Barbie standing on the side of the road.

Manoel leaned across and opened the door. After a moment's hesitation Barbie climbed in.

'I was just on the way to see you. . . .' she began, looking over at Laurel. 'If it's not convenient, though. . . .'

Once again she broke off, and Laurel shook her head swiftly. 'Don't be such a silly little goose. Of course it's convenient.' Her eyes twinkled. 'Escaping from parental intrigue again? That's why you were walking?'

Barbie chuckled and nodded. 'More or less, but I felt like a walk as well. Angel has been most unangelic all the morning.'

'Good. You can help me get tea – or better still you can entertain Manoel while I get it,' she added, and intercepted an amused side glance from Manoel. Matchmaking, she told herself sternly.

One good sign she discovered was that Barbie this time showed no reluctance at being left alone with Manoel. Her constraint had entirely disappeared and Laurel heard her chattering gaily as she paused outside the door, then she smiled, shut the door firmly behind her and went along to the kitchen.

When she returned, after an absence which she had deliberately extended because she wanted them to have time to get to know one another without anyone else around, Barbie was looking not merely cheerful but very much like a young woman who had made a discovery that surprised her. Her cheeks were flushed and her eyes several shades brighter than they had been before Laurel disappeared, and it was quite plain that Manoel had been taking the utmost advantage of the sudden precious opportunity with which he had been presented.

Laurel couldn't say for sure, of course, but she could have sworn that in that moment Barbie was giving little or no thought to Paul Brenton.

Laurel set the tea tray down on the table and smiled at the youthful ingenuousness of Barbie. Whenever she thought no one was observing her she glanced thoughtfully at Manoel, and it was plain from her glances that she was taking stock of all the little things about him that had escaped her before. She was, in fact, discovering the young Portuguese for the first time.

Mentally, Laurel chuckled to herself. Barbie might be too inexperienced to see through Paul Brenton's facile charm, but that also meant that she was too inexperienced to detect the careful trap into which she was now being led, and would doubtless not have a suspicion of it until it closed irrevocably round her. Manoel was beginning to exhibit signs of the Latin's sureness of touch when it came to matters romantic, and winning Barbie in particular.

CHAPTER EIGHT

TRUE to her word, Anthea apparently had no difficulty in finding people interested in the dance exhibition. They were all young, and one of them was a lovely Portuguese girl from the older part of the town, with fluid grace already in every movement of her slender body. After seeing her, as an afterthought and in case an unvaried programme of one particular style of dancing might prove monotonous, Laurel decided to enlarge it into an actual concert. Once again Anthea was sent off to use her powers of persuasion on likely performers. Secretly Laurel was a little surprised at the enthusiastic support received for both sections of the programme, but only time would tell whether it was due to genuine interest, intrigued curiosity because such a thing was novel on Ladrana – or pure and simple the unfailing Barrington methods of persuasion. Whatever it was, she found herself eventually in the unexpected position of being able to pick and choose her performers.

The only thing that did worry her a little was that all rehearsals took place at Castelanto. It had been against her will from the beginning, but, as Anthea had pointed out with irrefutable truth, the cottage was too small and the island would quite naturally expect Castelanto to be used, since the producer was supposed to be engaged to the owner. It need not have worried Laurel, though. Stephen hardly ever showed up. Sometimes she thought he even appeared to be avoiding her. She would turn suddenly, with a feeling of being watched, and find him standing in the doorway of the ballroom, but he would always incline his dark head with a faintly mocking smile and disappear with some remark about not interrupting her when she was busy. Everyone else accepted such an explanation, no doubt under the impression that they would meet after rehearsals were over, but it was always Anthea who drove her back to the cottage and Stephen never once came there.

She was hurt but quite resigned. After all, she had not expected it to be any different, once he had made up his mind. Quite obviously he had decided that he would risk allowing Roberta to come into his life permanently and now all he desired was to be freed from this fiasco of an engagement that prevented him entering into one nearer his heart. Laurel was beginning to feel the same way herself. The atmosphere was quite insupportable and the sooner it ended the better, whatever the aftermath was for her.

She was uncertain how to bring up the subject, and in the end it was Roberta who gave her the opportunity. The red-haired woman was far from being a fool. There was a quick and agile mind behind the cold green eyes that could turn soft only when she chose, and a completely selfish and self-seeking heart in the beautiful body. Roberta Fransom had come to Ladrana purely and simply to get back the man she had once possessed so completely. She did not intend to let anyone or anything stand in her way – certainly not an insignificant little schoolteacher.

She had always been suspicious of the amazing engagement that nobody had seemed to expect. It had happened too suddenly – and she had not forgotten the aghast surprise on Laurel's face at Anthea's announcement – too much surprise for it to have been caused merely by dismay at a premature announcement. She was convinced now that Laurel had not known of the engagement until it was made public. She had suspected it at the time, and subsequent careful observation had made her sure she was right. It all added up to just the answer she wanted, and having obtained her answer she was not slow to act upon it.

When Laurel received her invitation to Barbie's nineteenth birthday party she was by no means certain that she ought to accept. She wanted to go to the party herself, but quite obviously Stephen would be there, too, and they would have to continue the deception that was just about getting beyond her. If she had not already embarked upon arrangements for the concert she had the cowardly feeling that she would have dropped everything, returned his ring to Stephen by registered package, and turned her back on the island all in the same day. As it was, however, too much work had already been put into the concert for it to be possible for her to just drop it, and at least it was only a week away now. Immediately it was over the engagement could be broken officially, and she would make arrangements to return to England. Poor Ned would no doubt be upset, but that couldn't be helped. She *had* to get away from Ladrana.

Her decision reached, she felt better, and when Stephen and Anthea came over to fetch them in the evening she

173

was able quite calmly to respond to his greeting.

All the same, she was affected by the strong sensation that something was going to happen. She was keyed up and over-sensitive and a little fey tonight. Something was going to happen.

When they arrived at Mrs. Bertram-Smythe's large rambling villa quite a few cars in the drive proclaimed that they were by no means the first to arrive, and Laurel was not surprised to see that Roberta was among the guests, as well as everybody else from *Firebird*.

Barbie, a youthful, enchanting picture in white, was apparently resigned to being the centre of proceedings for the evening and gave only a rueful little grimace when Laurel came up to her. The usually unruly mop of curls was tidy and even decorated with a small spray of white flowers.

'Behold me on my best behaviour,' she said with a some-what wry chuckle.

'Whereas you would far rather be out climbing a tree,' Manoel put in from behind her.

'I suppose so.' She was strangely reluctant to turn to face him. 'I must be getting senile,' she added with a puzzled shake of her head. 'What with Laurel managing to rope me into her Greek dancing after all and now sub-mitting to being wrapped up in this stuff like an iced cake,' she finished inelegantly, with a rather disdainful flick of her fingers against the crisp white material of her dress.

'Don't try to deceive us,' Laurel countered with a laugh. 'You're beginning to enjoy it.'

'Guess I must be,' Barbie admitted ruefully, 'or I would have been out the back entrance long before this.'

Somebody appeared at her side and Laurel noticed that the young girl stiffened slightly. Paul Brenton held out his hand to her with his deliberately charming smile.

'May I have a dance with the birthday girl?'

Barbie hesitated, then she nodded mutely, while Manoel muttered something terse and sharp under his breath. Laurel watched them dancing together, the young girl and the experienced, slightly dissipated man, then she touched Manoel's arm lightly.

'Don't worry about it,' she said with quiet understanding. 'It will all come right in the end.'

Manoel shrugged. 'I suppose so – but I grow impatient.' He smiled suddenly, bending his dark head towards her. 'Will you dance with me, *pequeña*?'

'Sorry to break in on this little *tête-à-tête*,' Stephen's drawling voice said from behind them, 'but I think it's customary to have the first dance with one's fiancée.'

'But of course. Your pardon, my friend.' Manoel bowed with his usual courtesy and turned away to speak to somebody else, as Stephen put his arm around the taut figure of his fiancée and drew her on to the floor.

'That was rude of you, Stephen,' she said unequivocally.

He shrugged and ignored the remark. 'So Manoel grows impatient, does he? You'd better tell him he won't have long to wait now.'

'I think he knows that,' she countered – and decided that she had better be well away from the island when Manoel announced his engagement to Barbie, or Stephen was going to start asking a lot of awkward questions which she was going to find hard to parry. Of course he might just guess the truth without the need of asking them, which would be more than she could bear.

They danced in silence after that, a stiff strained silence that made her glad when the dance ended and she was able to return to Ned's cheerful, uncomplicated company.

For neither of them was it a good night. Anthea flirted continuously and outrageously with every man she danced with, and when Ned asked her to dance with him she pretended that she wasn't free. Ned accepted his rebuff without apparently being very much affected by it, but Laurel knew otherwise, and when long before anyone else took their departure he asked her whether she would like to leave she agreed with relief.

Stephen must have seen them go, but he made no attempt to go after them, or to say good night to Laurel.

When they got back to the cottage Laurel made coffee for the two of them, and they sat looking half wretchedly, half whimsically at one another in the kitchen.

So much for Barbie's party. Laurel knew that was what they were both thinking.

Preparations for the concert went ahead, and the week that Laurel was counting on speeding past her certainly did not drag. There was so much to be seen to, for which she herself was responsible. The costumes, the music, the performances of the various participants. . . . It was rehearsals, rehearsals all that week, and she had little time to think of herself and the miserable condition of her affairs.

The concert itself was to be held in the open, which seemed the natural setting for the Greek part of the programme. In a corner of Castelanto's spacious grounds there was a kind of natural grove in which the trees formed a sylvan background, and on a flat spread of turf before it the dances were to be performed. Rows of chairs facing this natural stage had been set out for the audience, and in place of a classical temple which they could not produce, a fallen tree-trunk and some branches of flowery foliage were their only props.

On the whole, Laurel was very well satisfied with the stage effects, and the finished costumes were very pleasing. It didn't seem to her that anything could go wrong, although Anthea elected to go on a picnic the morning before the dance, and it was a bit nerve-shattering hoping she would get back in time.

Laurel had had a week to steel herself for the comment that her broken engagement would cause when the news spread round the island, and for her the concert and the end of her engagement to Stephen were synonymous. Stephen had been treating her so cavalierly lately that she hoped she would have a chance to talk to him after the concert, and it was then she planned to hand back the emerald ring. He was quite unlikely to make a fuss – she knew that now – and even if he did it would make no difference.

Her mind was made up. . . . The farce had to be ended. But between her and the ending of it lay the agonizing couple of hours that were to be devoted to the concert.

They had a sketchy dinner and then Ned drove her over to Castelanto. The sky was beginning to darken and the coloured fairy-lights glowed amongst the trees. More of them had been strung up along the paths that led to the grove, and the whole effect was quite enchanting.

Stephen had gone into Milton to pick up the party from *Firebird*, and Laurel was also met with the information that Anthea had not yet returned.

She faced Ned with a worried look. 'I hope nothing has happened to her.'

Ned grimaced. 'Nothing ever happens to Anthea – not unless she arranges it.'

But another hour passed and there was still no sign of Anthea. Stephen came back from Milton and seemed disposed to be helpful, whether from sympathy because of her worried expression, or because he didn't want to disappoint his friends she had no means of finding out.

He personally escorted Roberta to the grove and saw her comfortably seated beneath the trees, then he returned to the terrace where Laurel was waiting with Ned and Barbie and the other members of the cast.

'Haven't you heard anything from Anthea?'

Laurel shook her head. 'Not a word . . . and she promised she would be here on time.'

'Any idea where they went?'

'No.'

'It's a bit hard to know what to do, then.' He frowned, rubbing his chin reflectively, and just at that moment the telephone rang stridently inside the house.

With a quick word of excuse Stephen turned and went into the house, leaving the others waiting anxiously for his return. Laurel could tell immediately from his expression when he rejoined them that it was Anthea who had telephoned. He looked a trifle worried, though, as he explained:

'Apparently they went to some god-forsaken spot for their picnic, then had trouble with the car when they started to come back. They had to walk until they could find somewhere to telephone from. Anthea is still hanging on, and she'd like a word with you, Laurel.'

Laurel darted into the house and picked up the receiver.

'Anthea, are you all right?' she asked.

'Of course I am, darling,' came Anthea's reply, but she hardly sounded as bright as she normally did. 'I'm so sorry, Laurel, but we can't possibly be back in time.'

'But what are we going to do?' Laurel wailed. 'We're on the point of starting.'

'You can do my numbers,' Anthea replied. 'You can do them far better than I could in any case, so no one will be deprived.'

Laurel agreed that of course she could do them . . . and then she remembered the final scene. Peter Marshall, who was with Anthea, would also have to be replaced.

'Use Stephen,' Anthea advised promptly. 'I used him for practising. In any case, he doesn't have to do any dancing, just stand around looking grim and preventing the girl making her escape.'

'Don't be ridiculous,' Laurel protested. 'I couldn't possibly—'

'It's the only way if you want the show to go on,' Anthea argued. 'I know it will be awkward under the circumstances, but you'll have to go through with it. You owe it to the audience.'

Even then, Laurel did not suspect that this was contrived. 'Where are you?' she inquired helplessly.

'Buldaro, a little mission settlement, miles from anywhere. We're lucky the mission is on the telephone, or I don't know what we should have done. Unfortunately their own car went into Milton to pick up some supplies and it's not back yet, so they can't help us. Stephen had better send out a car to pick us up,' she added, with all the assurance in the world.

Laurel turned to speak to Stephen over her shoulder. 'She wants you to send a car to pick them up. Is there any chance at all of getting them back in time?'

'Where are they?'

'Buldaro.'

'Buldaro? What in the name of Hades made them go right out there?' He nodded. 'All right, tell her I'll send a car.'

He turned away as he spoke, to give the necessary orders, and Laurel cut across Anthea's apologies to inform her that she had better ring off so that they could get the show started. Unavoidable as the accident seemed to be, she still felt that Anthea had let her down.

As she replaced the receiver, she turned to Ned. 'Just how far is Buldaro?'

'It took me a little over an hour to get there once, so we can maybe expect Anthea in about two hours.' He shrugged. 'Perhaps one of Stephen's cars might do it quicker, but the roads are pretty bad for fast night driving.'

'We'll just have to start then and hope for the best,' Barbie said. She slanted a quick glance up at Laurel. 'At least you know all Anthea's dances, since you taught them to her, so that's a help.'

'We still need Peter Marshall for the ballet,' Laurel protested, strangely reluctant to mention Anthea's suggestion that Stephen should be stand-in.

'Hm, that does complicate matters.' Ned ran his fingers through his thatch of hair ruefully. 'I'm afraid I'd be no good, pet.'

'Wait a moment,' Barbie said in sudden inspiration. 'I remember Anthea mentioning once that Stephen had been helping her with rehearsals. Perhaps he would. . . .'

She broke off uncertainly, catching sight of the extreme reluctance of Laurel's expression, but Stephen's drawling

179

voice finished the sentence for her.

'Perhaps Stephen would?' he suggested. 'In fact it seems the only way. The other two will never be back in time.'

'But I haven't rehearsed it properly,' Laurel protested.

'Brace up, my pet.' The laconic glance slid over her. 'You can always blame the mistakes on me.'

She tilted her head defiantly. 'What makes you think there will be any mistakes? I used to know it perfectly.'

'Well, perhaps I wasn't referring to that. Your reluctance to dance it with me might have another reason.'

She was somewhat surprised at the last remark, until she realized that the others had already gone, probably sensing something in the air.

She attempted a nonchalant shrug. 'What other reason could there be?'

'Well, you're the best judge of that.'

'Oh, you're ...' She broke off with an impatient gesture. 'We'd better get started.'

'Yes, perhaps we had – and I suppose I am impossible on occasion, as you were so kindly about to point out – but perhaps one day you'll guess the reason,' he added thinly and, gripping her elbow with almost cruel fingers, drew her along in the wake of the others.

After such an inauspicious beginning, the actual concert started off very well. The audience were all seated expectantly in their chairs and the little fairy lights slowly dimmed, allowing the moonlight to flood the grove. It was a full, golden moon, which was another reason why they had chosen this particular night for the concert.

The first item went off very well, with no hitch, the slow graceful movement of the old classical dance seemingly holding the audience spellbound, then the lights went up again to provide some contrast for the pair of young Portuguese dancers. There was the rattle of castanets and swift, tumultuous music after the slow dreamy beat of the previous one, then once again the lights were dimming and moonlight flooded the grove. This time Laurel had to almost push out a semi-hysterical Barbie, who protested that she could not possibly go out there in front of all those people and make a fool of herself, but go she did, a slender graceful little figure that lent a note of mischievous charm to the old movements.

At last Barbie came back, and it was at this moment that Anthea should have appeared, a radiant golden-haired vision, but instead a slender figure clad in yellow chiffon drifted out, swaying and bending in a manner that made her body seem boneless, so much so that even members of the cast, whom she had trained, gasped in surprise, because they had never seen her dance properly before, only illustrating some movement for their benefit. There was not a single sound from the audience. They seemed to realize the difference, too, and even Roberta Fransom watched as if compelled, because this was no insignificant little schoolteacher but a creature of fairy and almost unearthly beauty, as delicate as gossamer ... a dryad from the trees behind her, exulting in the freedom of the dance and holding the entire audience spellbound.

For Laurel, quite unaware of the effect she was having on the audience, there was no reality any more. She was lost to the world, enchanted, completely captivated by the magic of movement. And in such a setting it was not difficult to persuade herself that she had undergone some magical metamorphosis, and really was a thing of the woods, a sprite impossible to capture.

The music stopped, and the rest of the first half of the programme continued to charm the audience, and then they were shepherded back into Castelanto for refreshments while the glade was prepared for the final scene.

This was the one item for which somewhat impressive changes were made to the simplicity of the stage-set. In place of the fallen tree trunk quite half of the smooth grass was covered by a high platform that had been pushed into place and covered with imitation turf and small bushes. Below, the remaining space was filled with dancing red shadows by means of hidden lights with little disks revolving in front of them.

When the piece actually commenced the fairy-lights were extinguished again and moonlight took possession of the glade, until a brilliant golden light from a spotlight hidden in the trees created the illusion of sunlight and flooded the newly-erected stage. Laurel, assuming the identity of Persephone, daughter of Demeter, goddess of the earth, danced in the middle of this golden lake with the same happy abandon as before, and when the dark lord of the underworld appeared suddenly and swept her up from among her attendants and carried her down into the red shadows of the underworld she had no need to simulate fear. The expression on the face of Stephen, as Hades, the lord of the underworld, was positively diabolical. She was filled with a delicious frenzy of fear that was more real than anything she had ever felt before.

The golden light was swept away in a flood of cold white light as Demeter threw a mantle of winter across the land and the attendants that had been left behind pleaded for spring to return, while below them Persephone danced in the red shadows and strove vainly to elude her captor and reached the stairway that symbolized the way to the upper world. Slowly the attendants ceased dancing, to fall down exhausted by the cold winter, and Persephone sank down also, helpless and imprisoned, refusing all food save the pomegranate that she raised to her lips almost without realizing what she was doing, only to throw it away from her when she remembered her vow that she would eat nothing while she was held a prisoner.

Then Barbie came slowly down the grass-covered steps, holding in her outstretched hands the scroll that bore the ultimatum of Zeus, who was supreme amongst the gods of ancient Greece, that the prisoner should be allowed to go free ... but on condition that she had eaten some of the food of the underworld. Slowly Persephone picked up the pomegranate, her hope dying as she realized that she was trapped, but kindling into life again when she realized that her sentence had been commuted and that instead of remaining there for ever she would have to spend only half of her life in the dark halls of the underworld.

The music was particularly helpful at this stage, and even Barbie seemed to be caught up in the role she was playing as she moved towards Laurel, and the latter turned to follow her. But then Stephen's hand reached out and he caught at Laurel's arm and stopped her, while in his other hand he held the pomegranate, which was exactly as it should be. It was only when he pulled Laurel forcefully into his arms and held her with sheer brute strength and kissed her savagely that the script went haywire, and the rest of the cast looked on and gasped. But Stephen was not even bothering about the text of the dance, and he kissed Laurel again in the deliberate, punishing way that he had kissed on the first night that they met, and to her astonishment she, too, forgot the role she was playing and, despite the sheer brutality of his kiss, kissed him back and gloried in the complete primitiveness of this mutual exchange.

Afterwards, when she thought about it, she marvelled at herself. But not at the time. At the time, wishing he really was Hades and that she was Persephone, doomed to spend one half of her life with him, she could not have been more content.

And then reality supervened, and she gasped and tore herself out of his arms, and knowing what she knew about Roberta she wondered that she had not smacked his face publicly.

What happened during the rest of the dance was never very clear to her, but she knew that she moved as if everything was completely natural, and she succeeded in keeping well out of reach of Stephen's ruthless arms until the whole scene was over, and the audience was clapping enthusiastically in proof of the pleasure it had received.

Anthea had not yet returned, and as a matter of fact Laurel did not inquire for her, having realized perfectly long before this that her inability to dance the role of

Persephone herself that night was all part of a carefully laid plan. She had intended that Laurel should have to dance with Stephen ... and now that it was all over she was keeping well out of the way and no doubt hoping for some improbable result for her barefaced scheming that was unlike the actual aftermath as it could possibly have been.

The others all poured back into the house to change out of their costumes, and Stephen, too, vanished as if Hades' underworld had indeed swallowed him up. Laurel, her lips actually painful after Stephen's frenzied attack upon them, had no desire to come face to face with anyone until her fury of resentment had abated, and in particular she simply couldn't understand why she had been so weak in his arms. So she waited until she was reasonably certain the others would all have had time to change, and then entered the house by a side door with which she was fairly familiar by now, and made her way to the changing rooms which were fortunately quite empty when she reached them.

Hurriedly she changed out of her floating golden chiffon and into her own slender white dress, and after renewing her make-up and dealing with the attractive disorder of her tobacco-brown curls she descended the main staircase to look for Ned, whom she meant to implore to take her home.

She could hear a hubbub of laughter and voices coming from the great drawing-room, but there was no one in the hall. It was empty and echoing and deserted, and she was trying to summon up the resolution to face them in the drawing-room when she heard footsteps coming along a corridor behind her ... incidentally, the corridor which led to Stephen's private room.

'Can I speak to you for a moment, Miss Shannon?' Roberta Fransom's voice asked quietly.

Laurel spun round and stared at her. She was almost breathtakingly beautiful in a mature and elegant way, and her dress was a blaze of iridescent ornamentation.

Her flame of red hair made her white skin look whiter by contrast.

'Why – er – yes, of course.'

'It's cooler on the terrace. Shall we go out there?'

Laurel nodded mutely. She was feeling strangely exhausted after so much purely emotional dancing, and for the life of her just then she couldn't have found a voice.

She walked at Roberta's side across the hall and out through the main door on to the terrace. The lights of the house streamed out behind them, but the gardens seemed deserted, and it was very quiet on the stone terrace.

Roberta established herself on the low parapet, leaning against one of the upright pillars for support. She was smoking a cigarette, but she crushed it out and then tossed it over the parapet into the darkness of a flower border below them.

'I think this will do,' she said. 'I don't want to make a regular speech of this, and I see no necessity why I should go into details because of what I'm asking you to do. I think you are fully aware of the details, such as they are. Will you release Stephen from the ridiculous farce of an engagement in which you've involved him?'

Laurel put a hand out to support herself against the pillar. She heard Roberta repeating her request.

'Well? Will you?'

'Why should I?' Laurel's voice was a mere threat of sound, husky with weariness.

'Because you know very well that it is a farce, and right from the beginning it was never anything else.'

'I don't know what you mean,' Laurel said.

'I think you do, my dear.' Roberta opened her gold mesh handbag and extracted a delicate toy of a cigarette-case, from which in turn she extracted a cigarette. 'It was all caused by Anthea's meddling, wasn't it? She doesn't like me ... I know that perfectly well, but the young often take unreasonable dislikes, and Anthea is very spoiled.'

'Oh, really?' Laurel murmured mechanically.

'We all make mistakes, and I made mine long ago,' Roberta went on. 'But I paid for it – you can believe that or not, as you wish! – and now that I'm free I want to put matters right. I've come to Ladrana for that purpose, and if you knew me at all well you would realize that once I make up my mind I do not change it – not easily, anyway. And over Stephen I have no intention of changing my mind!'

'Have you told Stephen this?' Laurel asked, and she knew that in her heart she had been hoping against hope that she could keep Stephen – that even though they fought like mad, and he did not love her, she would eventually marry him. But now she knew definitely that she had been harbouring a pipe-dream. This really was the end, and she had no need to pack her bags and go all the way home to England in order to make it possible.

'Supposing I refuse to release him?' she asked in the same dull voice, before she could elicit from Roberta whether she had taken Stephen into her confidence or not.

'You wouldn't be so foolish, would you?'

'I love him,' Laurel said, and having said it it was as if she had made the one really important admission of her life.

Roberta's lips curved mockingly, cruelly.

'He doesn't love you.'

'How do you know?'

Roberta's eyes gleamed at her insolently.

'I do know. For one thing you're young and inexperienced, and Stephen is a very mature man.'

Recollecting his kiss only a short time before Laurel knew that, at least, was true.

'I shall grow older,' she answered quietly. 'And as I grow older I shall acquire experience . . . But you – if you forgive me for saying so – have left your youth rather far behind.'

'You little – bitch!' Roberta fairly spat at her. 'For that I'll tell you something that I intended to spare you.

Stephen doesn't love you, and he told me so. He's bored by you, secretly afraid that you'll never let him go, that you'll cling like a piece of ivy. . . .'

'Not poison ivy?' Laurel whispered.

Stephen stepped forward out of the shadows behind her – actually it was the deep shade of his own study window – and he spoke one word very forcefully.

'No!'

Laurel spun round and saw that he was standing almost at her elbow, Hades' sinister garb replaced by a gleaming white dinner-jacket, while his dark chin was thrown into prominence by the immaculate whiteness of his shirt-front, relieved by the neatness of his dark bow-tie.

'Not poison ivy, my darling. . . . Never, never poison ivy! The other kind, if you like, and you can cling to me as much as you wish.' His arm went round her, and he drew her nerveless body to rest against him. 'I think it was remarkably brave of you to tell this designing woman that you love me, and because she somehow managed to goad you into telling the truth at last I'll refrain from letting her know precisely what I think of her and merely ask her to leave us alone . . . and *never* come back to Ladrana and Castelanto!'

His voice was stern and cold, and so unlike any voice Laurel had heard from him that she shivered in uncontrollable alarm even while she allowed him to hold her with increasing tightness, as if he more than suspected she would break away at any moment, and that was the very last thing he intended to allow her to do.

'But, Stephen—' she began, in a small, uncertain voice.

'Not now, my precious,' he returned, while his free hand fondled her brown curls. 'The important thing at the moment is to deal with my old arch-enemy.'

'You must be mad, Stephen,' the woman hissed at him. 'I was never your enemy!'

'You came close to wrecking my life, and I don't intend that to happen again. I suspected when you turned up so unexpectedly that you were bent on some form of trouble, but I must admit it never occurred to me that you wished to renew our old association. If it had I would have taken the appropriate steps to safeguard myself, and to protect someone I love.'

'You can't possibly love such a little empty-headed—'

'Please go!' he requested icily.

Roberta Fransom had never felt so frustrated, or so furious, in her life.

'All right,' she declared venomously, 'you can have it your own way. But if she isn't empty-headed she has the mentality of a schoolteacher, and if you think you can live happily with a prim little schoolmarm then you're not the kind of man I once took you for. What sort of a life do you think you'll have with her organizing your every waking moment just as she organized the concert tonight?'

'It's a pity you hadn't the ability to take part in the concert,' he replied briefly. 'But then you're all on the surface, aren't you, Roberta? . . . and you always were! And I would remind you that the years are passing, and even the surface will not have as much charm a short while hence as it has at the moment,' he finished cruelly.

Roberta winced.

'You're a beast, Stephen!' she told him.

'Maybe,' he agreed, 'but I'm telling you the truth. If you don't like it the seas are wide, and *Firebird* is an excellent example of an ocean-going yacht. I should prevail upon your friends to put to sea in her at once, and then the atmosphere of Ladrana will be very much sweeter and pleasanter for everybody.'

She hesitated for one moment longer . . . then she turned on her heel and walked away from them.

Laurel looked up at the man who had made her his prisoner for the second time that night, and she protested because she felt she ought to do so.

'You were cruel, Stephen . . . and she's the type who will remain beautiful until she's quite old.'

'Will she?' He sounded completely indifferent.

Her eyes began to glow. They reminded him of over-bright stars peeping up at him from the protection of his arms.

'And I simply don't understand how you can prefer me to her,' she added, aware of sounding a little ungrammatical for a schoolteacher, but not in the least bothered by it in that moment because schoolteachers had been very comprehensively dealt with in the last few minutes, and according to Roberta they lacked something. 'That's to say, if you do prefer me to her ... really, I mean,' she said with sudden agonizing shyness.

'Little idiot,' he said softly, and smoothed her hair. It amazed her because his hand was trembling, and she could feel it. 'And what an absolute little idiot you are!' he said, cupping her face in his two hands and gazing at her as if he nevertheless had a distinct preference for little idiots. 'You don't seem to know when a man has lost his heart to you, and when his heart just tumbles out of his body and lies at your feet you're much more inclined to tread upon it than pick it up and thank the kind gentleman for being so susceptible.'

His arms fastened about her, and she felt as if every bone in her body would break as he crushed her up against him and addressed her with the utmost urgency.

'Don't you know I love you, Laurel? ... In a way I've never loved any woman before! And won't you please allow it to penetrate to your understanding that I'm never going to let you go! You're going to settle down here on Ladrana as my wife, and the mother of my children, and that is the fate in store for you!'

She felt as if her mouth was literally scorched as his kisses descended upon it thick and fast, and when she could no longer stand because her strength was draining away between her lips and the starry heavens above her were whirling round like a kaleidoscope she depended upon the sheer brute strength of his arms to keep her from sinking in a graceful, overcome heap to the floor of the terrace. But even so, she held him away from her for a moment, and she managed to ask the question:

'But why – *why* – did you treat me so badly in the beginning? If it's true that you loved me as soon as you saw me. . . .'

'*If* it's true! You appalling sceptic! How else did you expect me to treat you when you behaved as if you loathed the sight of me?' he demanded.

At this distance of time she simply couldn't believe it.

'But I loved you, too. . . . I must have done,' she admitted.

'Then all I can say is that we behaved like a couple of lunatics!'

There was another delicious interval of silence, and then she had another question to ask.

'Did you and Anthea arrange her absence tonight? I mean, it was arranged, wasn't it?'

'If it was I had no part in it – but I'll admit it was a jolly good idea.' He grinned at her through the shadows on the terrace. 'It provided me with an excellent opportunity to kiss you!'

She shivered in momentary unhappiness in his arms.

'But I was going to give you your ring back tonight,' she told him, 'and I was going away—'

'Then I can thank Roberta for interfering with your plans!'

She sighed suddenly.

'Poor Ned! Do you suppose Anthea has any feeling for him at all?'

'Give her time,' he advised. 'At the moment she's a butterfly, spreading her wings, but one day she'll need to settle somewhere, and then it will probably be Ned. But I wouldn't worry about either her or Ned, for after all, you were difficult and prickly enough, weren't you, my darling? – And I won in the end!'

Laurel settled blissfully against him. She couldn't honestly believe that she had ever been difficult or prickly, but if Stephen said so then she was prepared to accept that it was true, simply and solely because he was Stephen.